THE OPERATOR

A Bill Blake Novel

Rob Jones

"Dying ain't much of a living, boy."
Josey Wales, 'The Outlaw Josey Wales'

ONE

They murdered me at midnight. Or, at least they tried to. My own men's betrayal of me was something I could never forgive, but revenge came later. Of the enemy, two of the three bodyguards were dead less than a minute after we had broken in through the skylights. The third man was better and moved like he meant it. Tucking his chin down against his chest, he threw himself into a rolling dive and disappeared out onto the upper landing. He had a lot of places to run. This was a Georgian townhouse in Connaught Square, Central London. Five levels, six bedrooms. All owned by the Russian Government and used as a safehouse for upmarket problems.

I threw a stun grenade after the bodyguard, shielding my eyes when it lit up the landing. Gilmore was first through, spraying the cashmere wallpaper with rounds from his shortened C8 CQB carbine. Chambered in the 5mm NATO cartridge, the blast made short work of the bannister running around the top of the stairs but failed to take out the fleeing man. He had vaulted over the rail and dropped down to the next floor.

"Go, go, go!"

Gilmore made tracks, followed by Rollins and Foster. I checked the rest of the top floor was clear and then made my way through the smoke to the stairs, sweeping my carbine assault rifle from side to side as I went. Back then killing people was part of my job, and I was good at it. If you're like me, thinking about life and death isn't recommended. You just get on with the job. It's the second oldest profession in the world, but I take no pride in it. I never enjoyed it and I don't like to talk about it. But I'm no psychopath. Using that word to describe people who work in my line disrespects them and what they do. We're professionals.

I approached the bottom of the stairs and heard screaming. When I reached the front room I saw the final bodyguard dead on the floor and a woman standing beside a large fireplace with her back up against the wall. She was shaking with fear and I recognised her at once as the target. Gilmore, Rollins and Foster were in front of her, guns raised. I walked towards her and took a pair of cuffs from my belt. She would be in an MI5 interrogation suite in less than an hour. We had done our job and in record time too. Ninety-seven seconds from the roof to acquisition of the target and all three bodyguards down and out.

Then, Gilmore, a hard and decorated bootneck in a former life, opened fire on the woman right before my eyes. There was no hesitation, no pause. No moment to consider what he was doing. He squeezed the trigger and cut her to pieces, a premeditated cold-blooded murder that took my breath away.

"What the hell are you doing?" I yelled. "Our orders are to bring her into HQ!"

"No, no they're not."

"Yes, they are!" Foster said, turning to me. "I have no idea what the hell is going on, sir."

I was looking at Foster. He was wearing a black beanie and his face was covered in camo grease but the look of anger and confusion was clear to see. Now, I turned around and saw Gilmore approaching me. He was gripping his carbine in his hands and the trigger's selector lever was still switched to R, which meant semiautomatic fire. He was a big man with a short temper and hard to control, and when he padded over to me I moved to swing my weapon up.

He whipped his gun into the firing position in a heartbeat. "Whoa, chief. Leave her where she's resting and get your hands away."

The acrid smell of so many bullets being fired in the enclosed space hung heavy in the air.

"I don't think so, sergeant," I said. "I'm ordering you to drop your weapon, now."

Gilmore's face was steel. There was no chance he was going to obey me. I was his commanding officer but he had already stepped well outside the chain of command by killing Natalia Zakharova right in front of me. I was just playing for time, and he knew it.

"I'll kill you, Bill," he said. "Arms where I can see them or you're leaving this place in a bag. Now, drop the damned gun or I'll open fire."

"Do as he says, boss."

Rollins. I was shocked to my core. I had known both of these men for years and now they were betraying me. At least Foster seemed to be on my side.

3

Gilmore stepped closer. "Now, chief. Lower the weapon to the floor and then draw your backup very slowly and put it in the same place. Then the same thing with your blade. We don't want any problems here tonight."

I looked at Zakharova's cooling corpse. Her clothes were peppered in bloody holes and her dead eyes stared up vacantly at the ceiling.

"I think we already have a problem," I said.

"This is nothing like as bad as things can get and you know it. Do as I say."

The gun smoke was clearing. "Under whose authority?"

"I won't ask again, Bill."

I considered firing on him, but Rollins was the deciding factor. He had positioned himself at a wide angle to my right very deliberately. If I fired on one of them I wouldn't be able to sweep the gun around to the other before he cut me down like a dog. I lowered my gun to the ground. Then, I took off my tactical vest containing my backup pistol and dagger and gently dropped it to the carpet beside the close-quarter battle carbine. It wasn't what he'd asked me to do but it would be a hell of a lot easier grabbing the vest than scrambling to pick up separate weapons all over the floor.

"Kick them all away."

I kicked the carbine and the vest away with my boot.

Then, when Gilmore and Rollins were staring at me, Foster reached for his gun. Rollins was faster, firing a short, controlled burst into his chest. Even with the vortex flash suppressors on the end of their carbine barrels, the noise and light show in the enclosed space was savage. The rounds

4

blasted out through his back and he dropped down to his knees, his eyes burning with a sad desperate realization that his life was over. Rollins fired again, a double-tap to the forehead and Foster slumped down dead on the hearth, his face contorted with rage and fear.

"What have you done?" I said.

Gilmore said, "We've done our orders, Bill. That's what we've done." He walked over to the dead Russian bodyguard and picked up his weapon, a Vityaz-SN nine-mil parabellum submachine gun. "All that remains is tidying you up, but that little problem won't last for very long." He checked the weapon over and inspected the magazine before smacking it back into the gun.

"What's this all about, Roy?" I asked.

Gilmore said, "You came here tonight and killed this woman and her bodyguards, but not before this one right here," he prodded the dead man with his boot, "got a lethal shot off and killed you, too."

"And why would I do that?"

He shrugged. "I'm just following orders. I don't need to know why. All they told me was that what happens here tonight is vital for national security."

"Orders from inside D19?"

Gilmore and Rollins shared a quick glance before the senior man replied. "From way higher than that, Bill."

I paused a beat. "You can't think you're going to get away with this?"

"We already have done," Gilmore said. "They've probably already written your obituary."

5

I felt sick. Whatever this was, it had been meticulously planned to the last detail. I felt like I was way out of my depth. I changed tack. "How long have we known each other, Roy? Sixteen years?"

"More like seventeen, boss."

"And that means nothing?"

He shrugged again. "You know how it is. We play a tough game and we play by different rules. We know all this when we sign up." He checked his watch. "No more talking, boss. This is over. It's time to say goodbye now. I respect you, Bill. Always have done. But this is it."

It was a split decision and I made it without hesitation. I threw myself into a roll towards Rollins and Gilmore opened fire. I came out of the roll and rugby tackled Rollins to the floor, smacking his weapon away from me, wrenching it out of his hands and spraying lead all over the room. Gilmore and Rollins dived for cover and returned fire. They were blocking my path to the front of the house but I still had the rear. They speculated my next move and Rollins threw a grenade into the kitchen behind me.

It exploded with a savage intensity, blasting cupboards and countertops all over the room and instantly igniting the wood and curtain fabric. Rapidly, a serious fire began to consume everything in the obliterated room but it was my only chance. With one more rapid burst of cover fire, I reached down and snatched up my tactical vest. Then I turned on my heel and sprinted into the inferno at the back of the safehouse.

TWO

Like everything else in the room, the kitchen door was on fire, but I knew from earlier in the raid that it was unlocked. I aimed for it, jumping over flames and smoking debris as I reached out and grabbed the handle. Wearing my tactical gloves I was able to turn the handle down and pull the door open.

I tumbled out of the house onto a large patio and crashed into a cast-iron table, coughing and disoriented. Behind me, in the house, I heard Gilmore and Rollins shouting and more gunfire. Smoke was pouring out of the door and billowing up into the night air in a thick black column. Sirens now, flashing red and blue on the bare canopies of the plane trees at the end of the terrace. Fire and police emergency service vehicles were arriving mob-handed.

I tossed Foster's carbine to the ground, put my tactical vest back on, climbed over the side fence and landed in the neighbour's garden. Then I sprinted down the narrow alley at the side of his house, climbed over his gate, ran down his front steps and crossed the road, vaulting over the fence and entering the park at the centre of the square. Landing with a thud on the grass, I headed across the small park. Behind me, marked and unmarked police cars screeched to a halt outside the burning house. I saw no trace of Gilmore or

Rollins and guessed both of them were long gone into the night like a couple of phantoms. They were both very good at that.

Something big had gone down here tonight and if I was going to find out what, I had to tuck tail and run. I started by crouch-walking across the park and leaping over the wrought-iron fence on the other side. From here, I crossed the street and broke through another side gate on one of the houses opposite. Down the alley at the side of the house and through the back garden. Over the back fence and through St George Fields and then south on Albion Street until I emerged onto Hyde Park Place.

With the sound of sirens still shrieking behind me in the rainy night, I crossed all four lanes against the No Walking light and vaulted over the iron fence running around Hyde Park. This is the largest Royal Park in London and in here I was able to slip into the shadows of a clump of oak trees and take a breath. Things were moving fast. The sirens roared and I was still in the black combat fatigues I had worn for the raid, including the respirator. I dumped that but kept my ops waistcoat and the body armour. Two unmarked police cars were racing east along Hyde Park Place. They made a sharp left turn into Albion Street and there were no prizes for guessing what they were responding to.

I knew the city and I knew the park. I had walked here countless times with Emily back in the day. My head buzzed with escape routes, exit strategies. Without knowing what had just happened, or why, it was difficult to figure a way out. How long had this taken to plan? Who was behind it?

What did Gilmore mean about it being a matter of national security?

These were all questions for later and I had to move on. The best thing was to head south, skirting the north shore of the Serpentine and then get into Hyde Park Corner tube station. If I kept my mug away from Big Brother's CCTV cameras on the underground, I could get miles away in any direction I wanted and that would give me more time to think.

I started out, keeping to the shadows of the trees wherever I could and tucked my chin down into my chest and put my hands in my pockets. Nice and easy. As casual as you could get while wearing a tactical waistcoat stuffed with special ops gear. Luckily, it was after midnight and most people were at home. The chaos behind me receded into the night and then things went quiet. I walked past the bird sanctuary and the ranger's lodge without any trouble. It was dark and the park was locked and out of bounds to the public. Cutting down the east end of the Serpentine I was approaching Carriage Drive when I saw the lights of the underground station up ahead in the rain.

Then I saw them. Two black box trucks swerved to a halt on Carriage Place just south of the fence and a dozen armed men piled out of the back of them. Were they tracking me by infra-red reconnaissance satellite or had I been bugged with a GPS tracker before the raid? Maybe, but unlikely. I kept my gear out of the reach of others all the time. I kept my money on the satellite – another good reason to get underground as fast as possible. I turned and saw another bundle of armed men in black balaclavas moving towards me. They weren't my guys, for sure, but they were loaded up with submachine guns and stun grenades and respirators all the same.

I breathed out a long slow breath. Was the game already up? I thought so. Not even the possibility of diving into the Serpentine and going underwater for a few minutes before coming up out of sight was open to me – by now, a handful of heavily armed counter-terror police were blocking my only way to get there. But then I saw my chance. A car had pulled up at some red lights to my right, a hundred yards to the west of the box trucks. Slowly, a number of other vehicles began to pull up behind it and form a queue at the lights. It was now or never, so I bolted. They saw me flee and called out.

"Stay where you are!"

"Get down on the ground!"

I leapt over the iron fence and crashed down on the wet pavement with a hefty smack. They couldn't fire on me while there was any chance of civilians in the crossfire so I ran along the line of cars to the one at the head of the queue and wrenched open the driver's door. The man inside was middle-aged and wearing an expensive watch. He presumed it was a car-jacking, not totally unheard of in London these days, and started to pull his watch off. He said something in another language and waved the watch at me.

"Get out!"

He looked confused. Then, he cowered and pulled back. No time for words, I leaned in, popped open his seatbelt buckle, grabbed a fistful of his suede jacket and hurled him out of the car. Away back in the rain behind me, the armed men scrambled back to their box trucks and fired up the engines.

It was time to make tracks.

THREE

I slammed my foot down on the throttle and tore away from the red lights. When I checked the mirror, I saw them behind me. They were giving chase in the box trucks. Backup would be swift, including airborne, so I had to get away. That still meant an underground station but Hyde Park Corner was out. I knew the area well. Up ahead on the left was the Royal Air Force club and beyond that Green Park tube station. Whether or not I could reach it fast enough to get inside unobserved was another matter.

There is an art to driving at speed. An art to driving under duress. Obstacles bear down faster than you expect. Reactions must be sharper. Nerves tighter. You loosen your grip on the wheel and let it slide through your fingers like oiled steel. Listen to the revs and feel the engine. Quickly learn the limits of each gear and where the biting point is. If you're in front of the chase, then eyes always flicking to the mirrors. Roll with the chassis when you make a corner. Make the car an extension of your body.

The car I had stolen back at the lights was a fairly new Audi A4 Quattro. Six-speed manual transmission, improved cylinder head on an iron engine block, 220 horsepower, and a thick, rich torque whenever you want it. They're heavy but they have powerful engines and handle like a dream. I knew from experience in D19 that the box trucks behind me handle like couches on wheels. So, that was an advantage.

I overtook a black cab and raced along Piccadilly. It was late and the streets were quiet, allowing me to weave in and out of the light traffic as I moved east. Mirror check. The box trucks were still in pursuit and getting underground was more important than ever. Hyde Park Corner station was already long gone and Green Park was next up. It would be a non-starter if they saw me enter it and as I blew past Park Lane Hotel, the trucks were still too close.

I raced past Green Park and decided to put some more distance between me and the box trucks before aiming for Piccadilly Station. Then, the game changed. Gliding over the noise of the wet road I heard the distant crack of a gunshot and then the Audi's rear window shattered into a thousand pieces. Even though the traffic was almost non-existent, firing on a fugitive on one of London's most famous thoroughfares told me these guys weren't operating under normal procedure.

I had thrown Foster's carbine down in the garden of the house back in Connaught Square, but I still had my Glock 17. Black matte, rugged grip, milled stainless steel slide and a full magazine. I reached down and grabbed it with my left hand as I pushed the window down. The wind blew sheets of rain into the cab and the cold, rushing air struck my face like a slap. I rotated my upper body in the seat and twisted my arm around over my shoulder until the muzzle was pointing back at the box trucks. Then I fired, striking the windscreen of the leading vehicle.

It swerved to the side and allowed the other truck to overtake it. A soldier in the front passenger seat leaned out and fired on me with a Heckler & Koch submachine gun. Short, controlled bursts aimed at the rear tyres. Definitely not our guys, I thought. We'd dumped the HK for the Colt C8 some time ago. The rounds found their mark and both my rear tyres blew out, slamming the rear of the stolen Audi down on the ground. The exposed wheel rims grated along the tarmac in a shower of orange sparks and I struggled to bring the car to a safe stop, only narrowly avoiding several people standing around the base of the Eros statue in the middle of Piccadilly Circus.

Engine off, door open and out into the rain. I saw the glow of the underground station but it was too late. Two more box trucks were parked up outside it and more men were piling out of their rear doors, all heavily armed. A handful of civilians screamed and scattered as the men shouted at me to drop the gun. I knew the drill well enough and set the gun down on the pavement. Everywhere I looked, armed backup was arriving from all directions. A chopper appeared over the top of the famous neon sign on the northern side of the Circus and illuminated me with a powerful searchlight. Behind me, the smoking, steaming Quattro with two blown-out tyres wasn't going anywhere.

I was pinned down with nowhere to go.

"It's over, Colonel!"

"You're surrounded."

They drew closer in short, cautious steps. Guns raised and aimed at my head. They knew what they were doing and they were good at it. Submachine guns raised into the aim and moving towards me with fingers on the triggers. Not giving me time to think or respond. They screamed orders at me from all directions to confuse me and make me submit. I recognised the tactics. I had done them myself enough times.

"Down!" one screamed. "Get down, down, down!"

Three more appeared from the shadows, fanning out behind the others as backup. Scuttling forward like black beetles in the rain. Others came round behind me and cut off my access to the Quattro. More guns, their matte barrels glinting in the neon lights. Rain tumbling from the sky and down over my face. Hair slick with it. Behind them, ordinary uniformed police officers were directing the handful of pedestrians away onto side streets, arms spread out wide like wings to stop them from getting past.

"Hands in the air!"

"Get on your knees!" another yelled.

A second rushed up beside him, the stock of his Heckler & Koch MP5 neatly buried in his shoulder as he swept the barrel up into the aim and pointed it at my face. Then a third, fourth and fifth. Men barked orders into palm mics. Breath plumed into the cold air and radios crackled. I stared up at the cold rain falling from the sky and blew out a long, slow breath.

"Now!"

I fell to my knees and put my hands behind my head.

It was over.

FOUR

On the divide between Mayfair and Soho, West End Central Police Station was on Savile Row, not a million miles away from where they had arrested me. When we pulled up, I was bundled out of the van and into a side door so fast my feet barely touched the ground. They had already removed my tactical vest back at Piccadilly Circus so I was unarmed. Inside, I was transferred to another group of police officers. No one spoke. Things moved fast and I could tell they weren't going to waste any more time. Here, I was marched through a series of low lit corridors and pushed inside an isolated interview room.

The room was sparse. The walls were covered in chipped green paint and in the corner an old iron radiator clicked as it cooled down. A large interview table, some chairs. A small barred window was above head height and offered a view of a concrete wall and nothing more. I blew out a long, calming breath and tried to make sense of what had happened to me. I had no clue, but whatever it was had happened lightning fast. Less than thirty minutes ago I was descending a helicopter's rope ladder and blowing open the skylights of the house in Connaught Square. Now I was sitting in an interrogation suite in a secure London police station facing several murder charges.

I searched my mind for answers and came up blank, but one thing was obvious. I needed help and I knew where to turn. I had joined the Parachute Regiment straight after Sandhurst with an old friend and immediate superior, John Grant. The two of us met at college and had played rugby together there and we signed up for Sandhurst on the exact same day. From there, we were selected for P Company training and made it through the hill tabs and got to battalion together. Many years later, we transferred out of the Paras into the Special Air Service. He was first to pass selection into the Regiment. This took me longer, but I never gave up and made it six months after him. We became strong friends.

I knew I could trust John, and right now he was the only person I would trust. I didn't know who had set me up, but I knew it had to be someone inside either the British Secret Service or worse, the Regiment or even D19 where John and I worked. D19 was a small, unofficial cadre within the SAS Regiment, staffed by special operatives who usually ended up working alongside the British Secret Intelligence Service. I was not part of the SIS and couldn't begin to guess who might have set me up from within it. But D19 was different.

Only a handful of men were ever in D19 and my immediate sub-division was even smaller – me, John Grant, Mark Shepherd, Roy Gilmore, Ben Rollins, Andy Foster, Peter Brookline, a handful of other special operatives. But Gilmore had said his orders had come from higher. And he had said something about my death being necessary to protect the vital national interests of the country. I had no idea what that could mean. My thoughts were broken when a man in a smart grey suit stepped into the room and sat down opposite me at the big interview table. He was accompanied by another man in a suit and two uniformed policemen.

"Who are you?" I asked.

"You're in the custody of the Metropolitan Police, sir. You have been made aware of your rights, I take it."

"No."

"In that case, allow me to acquaint you with them. William Blake, I am arresting you on suspicion of murder. You do not have to say anything but it may harm your defence if you do not mention when questioned something you later rely on in court. Anything you do say may be given in evidence. Do you understand what I have just told you?"

I said nothing.

"I see. You have one phone call and I'd recommend you make it to a very expensive lawyer."

"And blow my chances of calling the talking clock?"

No response. He opened a manila folder and shuffled through some papers. "We'll start with the basics. Can you please confirm to me your identity for the official record?"

"I think not," I said. "At least, not until I've made my call to the talking clock."

The man sighed. "Very well, then. I believe you to be Lieutenant Colonel William Blake, Bill to your friends and acquaintances," he said, the words rolling off his tongue like oil. "Senior officer in the Parachute Regiment for fifteen years and then transferred into the SAS where you are a staff officer." A long pause as he shuffled the papers until they were all squared off again and then set them down on the desk. "Bit young for a colonel?"

"It's a half colonel," I said. "Not unusual at all. And I'm not a staff officer because that pleasure is reserved for full colonels."

He nodded, straight-faced. Uninterested. "Why'd you do it, Bill?"

I looked him in the eye and waited ten seconds before speaking. "And you are?"

He exchanged a look with his colleague. "Oh, I'm sorry. How rude of me. My name is Detective Chief Superintendent Sullivan of Scotland Yard." The other suited man got up and walked around behind me. I knew enough about police interviews to know they weren't usually conducted by a Chief Superintendent at this time of the night, even murders, but I kept my surprise to myself. "Thanks. A little courtesy goes a long way."

Some awkward shuffling and another brief look at one another. "Earlier this evening, you were seen by multiple witnesses leaving a property in West London inside which officers working for the Metropolitan Police discovered the dead body of a Russian woman by the name of…" He leafed through the file one more time. "Natalia Zakharova. She was some sort of diplomat."

"Who told you that?" I asked.

Sullivan bristled. "We ask the questions, Blake."

"And apparently, provide the clichés."

No reply.

"You're not going to speak to us about why you killed this woman, then?"

"Whatever's going on here seems to be several layers of atmosphere above your head, Chief Superintendent. So no."

"Very well." The unidentified man sighed behind me. "Then we'll do it the hard way."

With no warning, he struck me hard on the head and my world went black.

FIVE

I woke up in a cold cell as black as pitch. I was on the floor with my hands at my sides and my head thundered with pain. Whoever had dragged me into the room had just dumped me on the floor and then locked the chunky metal door behind them. I got to my knees and then up to my feet. I fought back a wave of nausea and dizziness from the blow to my head. A dim, greasy light the colour of rotten apples spilt in through a narrow slit of a window at the same height as the one in the interrogation suite. At least I knew was on the same level.

I wiped my blood-rimed lips and spat another wad of blood on the concrete floor. Pain was radiating down the side of my head and into my neck and shoulder, but I was still in one piece so I decided to look around my new home. Eight by eight feet with a single unlit lightbulb above my head obscured behind a small protective wire cage. Other than that, there were no other features. No table, no chairs. This is where they left you to sweat.

Or in my case, to do some more thinking.

Gilmore and Rollins had murdered Natalia Zakharova and her bodyguards and Andy Foster and then tried to kill me and frame me for their deaths. Gilmore was a good soldier but he didn't have it in him to plan an operation of this size. Someone else was doing that. Someone else was pulling his strings and it was up to me to find out who. The food chain moved up from Gilmore through me to my colleague Colonel John Grant and then up to our divisional commander at D19, Brigadier Peter Brookline. Neither Grant nor Brookline would ever betray me. This I knew in my heart.

The three of us had worked together for too many years for betrayal. We knew each other too well and socialised outside of work. Murdering each other wasn't something any of us would ever contemplate, no matter how dark things got. It had to be someone else. Someone outside of D19 as Gilmore had implied to me back in Connaught Square. I had to look higher, but that meant getting help from my superiors, Grant or Brookline. Maybe one of them could throw some light on what was happening to me but getting hold of them was easier said than done. If something involving the vital national security of the country really had gone down tonight, anything was possible. They might have gone to ground. They might already be dead.

I heard a key in the door and then it swung open. The man who had struck me in the interrogation suite stormed into the room with another man I had not seen before. They didn't look like policemen to me. One of them was holding a cosh and the other a bucket. It was no surprise when he threw the freezing cold water all over my face.

"Get up!"

I was already clambering to my feet when the man hurled the bucket to the concrete floor and slipped a hood over my head. I heard a chair scraping across the room and then they grabbed me by the shoulders and forced me into the seat.

"Why did you kill Natalia Zakharova?"

This was no police interview. I recognized the Special Forces interrogation techniques immediately and knew how I had to play it.

"Blake, Lieutenant-Colonel, 33942391, 17 August 1979."

"Let's not be silly."

I repeated what I had just said. Whoever these men were, they were not D19 or even SAS. I speculated if they might be former Special Reconnaissance Regiment men working in some capacity for MI5 or MI6. Nothing to do with me.

"Stop the bollocks, Bill. We know who you are and we know you killed Zakharova. What we want to know is why?"

I said nothing.

"All right then. Let me have a go. Earlier this evening you broke into a house in Connaught Square and murdered the Russian diplomat Natalia Zakharova."

"We both know I did no such thing."

"You did this because her status as a diplomat was just to cover her real identity as a member of the Russian secret service, an agent who was passing intel to D19 in return for British secrets and you wanted to silence her because she turned and started to blackmail you."

I made no response.

"We have evidence Brigadier Brookline of D19 is having a sexual relationship with Zakharova. Is he passing her intel?

Did he want her out of the way? Is that why he ordered you to kill her?"

"Speak to my agent."

He punched me in the side of the head and knocked me out of the chair. I crashed into the floor with a smack and nearly passed out. I fought hard to regain consciousness and just managed to hang on. From inside the hood, I heard shoes scratching around on the concrete floor.

"You're lucky I'm being so agreeable, Blake. As it turns out, you're off to the big house for further interrogation. I wouldn't want to be in your shoes. The best thing you could do is confess to the crime and be grateful for a very public trial and then a life sentence."

"Tempting, but what if I refuse?"

"Not my call. But word is, you and everyone you have ever loved will be killed. Confess now and save the bother."

"Where is Sullivan?" I asked.

He ripped the hood off my head and I blinked in the low light. The other one grabbed me and pulled me back up onto the chair. "There will be zero cooperation until you confess."

"I will under no circumstances confess. If you know me then you already know that, so why go through all this?"

"Like I just said, Blake, two monkeys are coming in here and lifting you for the murder. Just make it easy and confess and they might throw in a cup of tea when you get to your cell."

"Red caps?"

"They're on their way, so stop wasting my time."

Without warning, he lunged forward and threw a fist at me. I dodged my head to the side and fell off the chair for the second time. The other one padded over to me and grabbed my shoulders once again. He was trying to get me to my feet while his associate pulled himself up and then rushed me. I pulled back my arm and fired my elbow into the face of the man holding my shoulders. He fell back, grunting in pain and paused to check how badly his nose was broken.

Badly, as it turned out, and things were speeding up. The other guy was in front of me now and firing a jab up into my jaw. I sidestepped. He missed. I piled a fist into his face and knocked him down on his arse and then the door swung open and two soldiers stumbled into the room. Red caps. Royal Military Police. I didn't stop to think. I charged the man in the lead, struck him in the face with a quick jab and hooked his legs out from under him. He passed out and crashed to the floor and Sullivan burst into the room, startling the other red cap. I seized the moment, jumped over the unconscious soldier and grabbed the other one by the neck and pushed him up against the wall.

Sullivan and the two men in suits formed a semi-circle around me.

"Let go of him, Blake," Sullivan said. "You can't get out of this one."

Slowly, the three men closed in on me and I was quickly running out of ideas.

SIX

Time slowed to a crawl. I stood over the unconscious RMP's body, a boot on either side of his midriff, and gripped the other red cap by the throat, pinning him up against the concrete wall. The two suits looked mildly alarmed and Sullivan mumbled some words to a sergeant in the door. The sergeant turned and fled through the open door. He looked glad to be getting out of there.

"That was a very silly thing to do, Blake," Sullivan said. "You have no idea just how much shit you're in right now, and you just dug yourself down another six feet."

The two men in suits were standing by at my sides and the red cap's face was turning purple. Both his hands were still struggling to pull my arm away from his throat. I squeezed tighter but talked to Sullivan.

"You have no more idea what's going than I do," I said. "Admit it. This is a stitch-up."

"You're being paranoid."

"Am I? How many times does a man dragged in for murder get grilled by a Detective Chief Superintendent at this time of the morning? Who sent you in here, Sullivan? Who are these two men? They're not police."

Sullivan pulled his phone from a pocket. "Just let go of the soldier, Blake. There's a good man."

26

"Not until I speak with my CO."

Sullivan sighed. "Again, let's not be silly."

"Get him on the phone right now or I choke this man to death. It won't be the first time I've done it."

Sullivan looked at the red cap, still straining to talk as he clawed at my grip around his throat.

"Well?" I said, squeezing harder. The young soldier's eyes were bulging in their sockets and he was gasping for air in rapid, hoarse croaks. "What's it to be?"

He paused a beat and ran a hand through his hair. Silver in the temples, receding up into his forehead in a widow's peak. He looked at the red-faced RMP and winced. Then he looked at the two men in suits. One of them nodded. "You talked me into it. Who do you want to speak with?"

"Just get me a phone and I'll make the call."

The red cap stopped scratching at my grip. His arms fell down and hung loosely at his side.

Sullivan's nerve was breaking but he worked hard to look defiant. "I'm not happy with that arrangement. I make the calls."

"Wrong. I make the calls. I'm already killing this man. He's gone in another thirty seconds."

"Just let go of him, Blake," said one of the men in black. "You've made your point."

I ignored him and kept my eyes fixed on Sullivan. I was sure he knew about as much of all this I did. Plus he was the weakest link in this room. "You'll get me the call?"

He gave a reluctant nod. "Just let go of the soldier."

"No, phone first."

Sullivan reluctantly handed me his mobile phone and I let go of the man. His body slumped down to my boots and I made the call to my CO, Brigadier Brookline. The line was dead. Cut. This was new. I had called him only yesterday to organise a meeting about the raid. Not a good development. Had they already got to him? I made my second call and a man answered. A voice I didn't recognize.

"You're not John Grant," I said. "Who is this?"

"This is Michael Bentinck," a smooth, rich voice said.

Sullivan and the two men in black suits were listening intently. My eyes narrowed in concern. "Who are you? I thought I called John Grant's phone. I could have sworn it, in fact."

"All numbers from D19 have been redirected to my office."

"That's very generous of you, Michael, but I'm still waiting to know who you are."

"First, I'd like to know your identity. I don't recognise this number, and neither does my tracking software."

"Blake."

"Ah, as expected."

"What's your role in this, Bentinck?"

"I'm SIS. I've worked with Grant in the past."

Secret Intelligence Service, interesting but not surprising. The problem was, 'SIS' was an umbrella term for a massive, sprawling organisation. He could have been a part of any of it. Or none of it. I said, "Care to tell me what's going on here tonight?"

His voice grew more serious. "I'm mostly in the dark. I know something went wrong on an unapproved D19 mission in London and a Russian diplomat named Natalia Zakharova is dead."

"Unapproved?" I said. "It was a fully approved and official operation. And Zakharova was no diplomat, as I think you know."

He ignored me. "I know a D19 man was killed in the firefight along with an undisclosed number of Russian special forces soldiers working as bodyguards for the FSB. I also know you are going to be charged with their murders. Listen to me very carefully, Bill. From one old soldier to another. You need to abscond, and in a hurry."

Outside the interrogation room, I watched a number of uniformed police constables gathering with tasers and batons. Word had got around the station about what was happening. "Risky."

Bentinck continued. "I know they're listening. I know you can't say much, but if you want to survive this you need to get away."

"You mean to become an outlaw."

"Your words, but they add up to the same thing."

"Where is Grant?" I asked.

"I don't know. He fled an hour ago."

"I want to talk to John Grant."

"Then listen carefully. You must meet a man named Wainwright. He is an agent working for me who knows where Grant is."

"Where and when?"

"Arthur on 1 March. Grant said you'd understand."

He ended the call and Sullivan reached his hand out.

"Phone, now."

I handed it to him and things moved fast again. The door behind him widened further and two more RMP soldiers stepped inside. They were both armed with tasers.

"We don't want any trouble, Colonel," one of them said.

I raised my hands and stepped towards them. The men in suits stepped away from me. A bad sign. Sullivan also moved back into the corner of the room and started to make a call. He was talking to someone about my transfer into military custody. Then I did what I had to do. I brought the back of my hand up and struck the new RMP soldier in the face, reaching down for his taser. I tore it from his holster and aimed it at the other guard but it was too late.

The man fired his taser and a second later the electrodes' barbs pierced through my sleeve and flashed a pulse of fifty thousand volts up my back and around my body. It hurt like hell, a burning inferno of electrical pain crackling all over my skin and up my neck. Muscles all over my back spasmed and then I seized up, releasing the other red cap's taser and collapsing down onto the concrete floor.

I had no chance to recover. Less than a second after I had slumped down onto the floor, the other RMP and the suits were all over me, wrenching the electrodes off me and grabbing my arms. One of them yanked my hands roughly behind my back and I felt the cold steel of his Hiatt speed cuffs against my wrists. Then I felt a boot going into my side, blasting the air out of my lungs. I coughed violently and then another boot went in.

"That's enough!" Sullivan shouted. "I don't know what the hell goes in military prison, but this is a civilian cell and it's not happening in here. It was bloody bad enough you knocked him out during the initial interview. That's going to take some explaining."

The suits ignored him. One of them straightened his jacket and tie and screamed at the RMP. "Get him to his feet and get him outside to the van. I'm sick of looking at his ugly mug."

The men hauled me to my feet and bundled me past Sullivan into the corridor. Time blurred. I felt rain on my face and saw street lights streaking in the sky above my head. Then, I was in the back of a Land Rover Defender with an assault rifle in my face. The suits were gone now. It was just me, the two RMPs and a corporal in camos who was holding my tactical vest casually in his right hand. Property of the British Army. He tossed it into the front of the Defender and climbed in beside it. Then he fired up the engine, drove us out of the police station, made a couple of right turns and headed east.

"You're taking me to the Glasshouse, I presume?"

The Glasshouse is a term used by the British Army to describe a military prison. Tonight, I was talking about the Military Correction Training Centre in Colchester, Essex, just north of London. The place had a notorious reputation. I guessed it was where they had been ordered to take me because the charges were that I had broken not only the law of the land but British military law.

The RMP I had addressed said nothing. This was strange. Even as a prisoner, I was still a half-colonel. Through the eyes of a twenty-year-old private, this was not too many rungs below God himself. Instead, he and the man next to him exchanged a furtive look and shifted uncomfortably on the bench seat opposite me.

"I asked you a question, private."

"We're going to Colchester," said the corporal driving the Defender. "But you're not."

"Then where?" I asked. "And under whose orders are you operating tonight? I want names."

The Defender was cruising along the north bank of the River Thames now, still heading east. Neither man answered me, and now one of the RMP soldiers in the back turned his weapon on me. This was a major breach of army safety protocols. It could mean only one thing but I didn't wait to find out if I was wrong. I sprang to my feet and lunged at the man pointing the automatic rifle at me. Shoulder barging into him, we both crashed off the bench seat and onto the floor.

The other guard rotated on the bench seat and aimed his gun at us. He didn't fire. It was dark in the back and he didn't want to hit his colleague. The corporal at the wheel twisted in his seat and yelled at the soldiers.

"Take him down!"

The soldier took advantage of my cuffed hands and soon got on top of me. His gun had slid under the bench seat but he made do with his hands and started pummelling my face. I dodged one of the blows and forced him to miss me. He rammed his fist straight into the riveted floor under my head, splitting open his knuckles.

He grunted in pain and I seized the moment, forcing him off me with a headbutt and then pulling my cuffed hands up under my backside. At least now they were in front of me. I snatched the automatic rifle from under the bench seat and fired on both the soldiers sitting in the back of the Defender with me. Controlled bursts as I swept the muzzle from side to side until they were dead.

The corporal swore loudly and nearly lost control of the vehicle. As we swerved across the road towards the other lane, I saw him reach down to a holster. He pivoted around in the seat and the orange street lights glinted on the matte barrel of an army service pistol. I didn't hesitate and fired the automatic rifle through the back of his seat. The rounds punched a line of holes through the leather and spat clouds of cotton batting into the air. The corporal cried out in pain and slumped down dead against the steering wheel.

I looked through the windscreen and saw we were driving along a bridge crossing the Thames. We had veered fully onto the other lane now and the headlights of another vehicle were rapidly approaching us. Their lights flashed and the horn sounded. They tried to swerve out of the way but skidded back to avoid a collision with another car. With time running out fast, and my hands cuffed together, I clambered over the front seat, pushed the dead driver out of the way and grabbed the wheel just seconds away from a high-speed collision.

SEVEN

I spun the wheel hard to the right but the heavy Land Rover Defender was slow to respond and even with the brake pedal on the metal, it wasn't enough to stop the crash. The rain had made the road slick and the heavy military vehicle was skimming uncontrollably across it, spraying up great high arcs of water behind its tyres. Seconds later, the collision wasn't head-on, but driver's headlight to driver's headlight.

Each car crunched into the other, front wings crumpling with the force of the impact, but the other vehicle – a brand new Mercedes – got the worst end of the deal, spinning around in a high-speed arc of ninety degrees and crashing through the safety barrier on the west side of the bridge. I checked up and down the bridge and saw no other cars on it. Not uncommon for so late at night but it wouldn't last for long. Within seconds I'd have a dozen cars pulling up to rubberneck and see what had happened.

As the Merc's back end hung over the side of the bridge, I brought the smashed Defender to a juddering halt and slammed into reverse gear to get back to the scene of the accident. It was too late. The big black Merc had fallen off the side of the bridge and crashed into the north shore of the Thames.

A wave of emotions flooded over me. I had to go. I had to leave the scene as fast as I could before whoever was hunting me tracked me down. But I couldn't leave someone to drown in the river. I smacked my hand down on the wheel, found a set of keys on the corporal's belt and unlocked the handcuffs and then I opened the Land Rover door. At least it had finally stopped raining.

Jogging through the broken glass left at the scene, I peered over the side of the bridge and saw the Merc. It was still visible, but slowly sinking into the river. I had to act fast. This part of the riverbank was used by people mudlarking or picking over the mud for lost valuables. The ground was soft and the car was slowly sinking below the surface. I climbed over the side of the bridge and down the support struts until I was low enough to jump down onto the shore. When I reached the water, the main body of the car was out of sight with only the windows visible.

I plunged my hand into the cold water, found the Merc's door handle and wrapped my fingers around it. The car was slowly sinking deeper and the water was creeping up the side of the glass. Much higher and the pressure of the water would make opening the door impossible. That would mean wasting valuable time looking for something to smash the window, so I raised my right leg and thumped my boot down on the side of the car's rear door to give me more leverage.

I squeezed the handle open and heaved the door open against the weight of the cold water. It was hard at first, but the job got easier when the water rushed into the narrow aperture between the door and the sill. I leaned inside now, pushing against the top of the door with my right shoulder and reaching down over the driver to unbuckle her seatbelt. Young, in her late twenties, dark hair, slim and pale but her face was hidden by the darkness inside the cab. She was barely conscious despite the deployment of airbags. The impact of the crash had thrown her bag off the seat beside her and into the passenger footwell, and a dozen cigarettes and a red lipstick tube and a half bottle of vodka were floating around in the ankle-high water.

I tugged at the seatbelt and released it, letting it wind back through the sash guide and into the grey plastic end retractor at the side of her seat. I pushed my hands under her arms and lifted myself towards her until both our bodies were halfway out of the car. Then, I pulled her up over my shoulder until she was in a fireman's lift and backed away from the sinking vehicle. The temperature had dropped since the crash and the steam that had poured from the burst radiator before it went under the surface was hanging like smoke above the river.

Cars were starting to accumulate on the bridge above us. How much longer before the police responded to a call about the accident? I had to work fast and waded through the cold brown water with the woman over my shoulders. My breath condensed in the cold air as I made my way back to shore. When I got there, I had to step through a thick stretch of mud and through rusted safety bollards before finally reaching dry land. Lowering the woman to the ground, I saw her face clearly for the first time.

Maybe early twenties, I thought now. Dark red lipstick smeared across the bottom of her face. Tangles of wet brown hair covered much of the top part of her face and wound around her neck like a choker. I saw a split lower lip, a fresh cut just below her cheekbone, and a soft purple bag was forming around her left eye. It was difficult to see how she had injured herself this way in the crash. She had been wearing a safety belt and the airbags had deployed. I knew her head had not struck the steering wheel.

I was pretty sure she hadn't swallowed any water, and that was important. I checked her pulse and it was steady. Then, when I leaned in to resuscitate her, she started to come to. I pulled back, noting the strong smell of vodka on her breath. If she had emptied the bottle in the car she would be several times over the limit and in no state to drive. The accident was starting to make sense.

She opened her eyes and blinked. "Who are you?"

When she spoke, the breath condensed into wispy tendrils in the air between us.

"I'm the guy you nearly just killed."

She sat up with a jerk, leaning on her elbows as she tried to pull away and the sleeves of her denim jacket rucked up a bit. I saw a tattoo of a butterfly on the inside of her forearm, down by her wrist.

"Take it easy," I said. "I'm also the guy who just pulled you out of a sinking car."

She blinked again, desperately trying to focus her eyes on me. "Wait, what?"

"You were in a car crash," I said quietly. "Well, *we* were. You hit my Land Rover. You swerved off the bridge and crashed into the Thames. You were going under pretty fast and you're lucky to be alive."

"Shit, what about the car?"

"You need a new one."

The woman sat up and coughed. She was shaking her head and starting to tremble. At first, I thought it was shock, but when she spoke, her voice was thinner and scared and I got another idea. "He's going to kill me for this."

"Who's going to kill you?"

"Luca."

"Luca?"

"Luca Antonescu, my boyfriend." She raised a shaking finger and pointed at the Merc. The Thames had nearly swallowed the entire vehicle now and only the very top of the shiny roof was left, surrounded by a ring of air bubbles popping on the water's black surface. "That's his car. He's out looking for me now."

I nodded in understanding but said nothing. From the vodka bottle, the black eye, the split lip and the cut on her cheekbone, I was starting to form an opinion about Luca Antonescu.

"Let's go back to my Land Rover," I said, aware of the circus gathering on the bridge. "We can put the heater on and I'll drive you home."

She stood up now, a little unsteady at first. She nearly fell over, but I grabbed her arm and steadied her.

"Maybe a hospital might be a better idea," I said.

"No, no hospitals."

I helped her over to the shore and up the long way to the bridge. Most of the drivers had taken all the photos they wanted of the crash and were moving on. We walked over to the Land Rover and I asked her to wait for a second while I climbed inside and dragged the corporal's body into the back over the front seats. Not an easy thing to do, but she was scared enough as it was and I couldn't just leave her out here, drunk and with this Luca on the prowl. I covered the bodies with an old tarp, then I opened the passenger door for her and helped her inside. When I got into the driver's seat, I leaned over her and pulled out the vehicle's first aid kit. They always carry one on board. It's regulations.

I opened it up on my lap, turned on the engine and fired up the heater. It was an old model but the heater was fast and efficient. Seconds later, we both felt much better. Then, I checked the mirror and saw blue lights flashing behind us and the sound of sirens filled the air once more.

"We have to get out of here," I said.

"We can't leave the scene of an accident. It's against the law."

"We'll talk about that later." I hit the gas and drove towards the south end of the bridge.

"Wait a minute." She looked at me, still kind of groggy. "Are you a cop?"

"No."

She looked around and blinked. "Then, what's with the police Land Rover?"

"It's not police, it's military police. And a long story. Let's just say I borrowed it."

"You stole a military police car?"

I said nothing as I cruised off the bridge and we drove in silence for a few minutes until I pulled onto an anonymous side street on the south bank.

"Why have we stopped?" she asked.

"I'm going to clean up your face."

"There's no need, really."

I snapped the cold pack to activate it and handed it to her. "Here, hold this on your black eye."

"Whoa, how is this thing so cold?"

"You've never seen one before?"

She shook her head.

"When you snap it, you mix the water inside with a little tube of ammonium-nitrate fertilizer. It creates an endothermic reaction. Temperature usually falls down to just above freezing for maybe ten minutes or so. Should help with the swelling."

She lifted the pack to the side of her head and gently pressed it against her swollen skin. "If you're not police, are you a doctor or something?"

"No, I'm not a doctor. Just hold the pack to your eye while I clean up this mess."

She did as I told her and I cleaned her cuts with one of the sterile gauze pads. Then I handed her a plaster and told her to put it on the cut on her cheekbone. "The one on your lip can't be helped."

She took the plaster. "Thanks."

41

I closed the first-aid kit and twisted in my seat as I tossed it in the back. "So, home then," I said. "Where's that?"

"You mean you're not going to call the police?"

I shrugged. "I don't see any reason to. Do you?"

She was quiet for a long time. Some people hate silence, but I had learnt to live with it a long time ago. I liked it. It gave me time to think and right now I was thinking about if this woman had anywhere safe she could sleep tonight.

"Thanks for not calling the police," she said at last. "That would make things a lot more complicated."

I peered through the darkness at the smooth, silent surface of the Thames at the end of the side street. Silent when we crashed, maybe, but now the whole area was crawling with police and paramedics. "Good job I was the only witness."

"Yeah."

"What are you going to tell Luca about the Merc?"

"I don't know."

I fitted my seatbelt. "You buckle up, too."

Once again, she did as I said. She was still tense and frightened, but not of me.

I revved the Defender and pulled off the side street. "You never told me where home is."

She pointed to the right. "Just drive that way. I'll tell you where to go. I'm Laura, by the way."

"Hi, Laura."

"And you are?"

"Most people just call me Blake."

EIGHT

I cruised the Land Rover slowly through the mostly deserted city streets, slowing for each turn in case Laura told me to take it, but she never did. After a few minutes, I broke the silence. "You have nowhere to go."

"That's not it."

"I know you didn't get those cuts in the crash."

She looked at me, then turned her face towards the window. "I don't know what you're talking about."

"You can drop the act. I know what a fist does when it makes contact with a face. I've seen it many times before. On my face and the other guy's."

She paused a beat. "All right, you got me. Congratulations. I hope you feel clever."

I decelerated to take a shallow bend, then stamped on the throttle and powered back onto the next straight. This part of the city was all tower blocks and concrete flyovers and overhead railways. Old, and dirty and abused. The Defender's diesel engine drew us deeper into its heart with a low, satisfying grumble. I glanced at her reflection in the side window and the shape of her face reminded me a little of my wife's.

"Has he been doing it long?"

"I don't remember. It seems like forever."

43

"You remember where you live yet?"

"Not yet."

I changed up into the next gear and accelerated until the vehicle was running at a higher-pitched hum. I liked driving in the city at night. Quiet, smooth roads. Stop lights that flick to green when they sense your car rolling up at them. Counting the lit windows to see who's still up at one in the morning.

"Tell me, how does Luca bring home the bacon?"

"This and that."

"Unemployed?"

"Are you sure you're not a copper?"

"I'm not a copper."

"Not a doctor or a policeman," she said. "I'll guess it eventually."

"It's no secret. I was in the army."

"But not anymore?"

I suppressed a sigh. "No, not anymore. I left very recently. Minutes ago."

Another minute passed. Lights from a nightclub spilt out on the asphalt where two drunk men fought, but we just cruised straight past without slowing.

"What did you do in the army?"

"This and that."

"All right," she said, a smile creeping on her face for the first time. "Luca's a businessman, happy?"

"Not particularly," I said, flashing her a quick smile in return. "You see, I don't really care that much about your boyfriend's career."

"You asked."

I checked the rear view mirror. "All right, you got me. That makes us even."

"Were you in Afghanistan?"

"Yes."

"And Iraq?"

"Yes."

"SAS?"

"Why do people always ask that?"

"Well?"

I nodded.

She said, "Sounds exciting. I thought you guys were not supposed to tell anyone you're in the SAS?"

I shrugged. "We normally don't tell anyone we're in the regiment except very close family, but tonight I'm making an exception."

"For me?"

"Because I'm not sure I'm even in the regiment anymore. I don't know what's going on."

"I once went out with a bloke who said he was in the SAS."

I cocked my head and grinned. "Name?"

"Darren Gillespie."

I thought about the men back on base at Stirling Lines but the name meant nothing. "No, I don't think so. When?"

"Last year."

"No way. There are less than five hundred men in 22 SAS right now and I don't recognise that name. Sorry to break it to you, but he's not at Hereford. I think your ex is a Walt."

"A what?"

"A Walter Mitty, a fantasist. They pretend to be in the army for kudos. Yanks call it stolen valour."

"Doesn't surprise me. He was a real bullshitter."

"Sounds like it."

"He was in the army though. I saw the pictures."

"I'm sure he was, and maybe he even tried to get through selection."

"Yeah, he talked about it a lot."

I laughed. "The SAS isn't how people imagine it. Soldiers trying to get in the regiment need to focus on training and keep their yaps shut. Worse thing to do is talk about it. If you want to get into a regiment like the SAS then best keep it well under your hat. Deeds, not words. Do the right thing and you get noticed. Then, make your move."

"That doesn't sound like Darren."

"No."

She sighed and pulled a crumpled packet of cigarettes from her denim jacket pocket and lit one up. Blowing a long column of smoke into the car, she offered me one.

"Thanks," I said. "You're too kind. I thought these got trashed in the crash."

"Different pack."

I caught the tip on my lip and held it while she lit it up. The tobacco shreds shone in the dim glow of the instrument lights and she snapped the lighter shut with a metallic click and put it back in the pocket with the cigarette packet.

"What was it like. Afghanistan I mean?" she asked.

"Dry, dusty and dangerous. That's my review of Iraq, too."

She sank into the seat and tipped her head back against the rest. "Better than spending your whole life out in the sticks where I grew up."

"You're not from London originally?"

"Nah."

I got the impression she wasn't looking for sympathy, but really meant it. I could understand that. There were a lot of people in a lot of small towns who wanted to know what was over the horizon, but not all of them made it. In my experience, most of those that did were disappointed by what they found there. Wanderlust and nostalgia were two ends of the same rope. I took a long drag on the cigarette and thought about that until she broke the silence.

"You said you left the army a few minutes ago. What did you mean by that?"

I huffed out a weary laugh. "Forget it. My personal circumstances seem to have changed somewhat rapidly, that's all."

"What does that mean?"

"It means I think I just got thrown out of the army on my arse."

She muttered a quiet curse. "I'm sorry. I shouldn't be asking stupid questions."

"It wasn't a stupid question."

She smoked quietly, glancing at the cuts on her face from time to time in the reflection of the dark window. I knew what she was thinking about. She was scared to go home and

47

tell Luca about the Merc ending up in the water. There was no way she had driven very far when she hit me back on the bridge, so we were already way past wherever she called home.

"You want me to take you to a hotel?"

"No, but thanks. I have to face him sometime, so I may as well get it over with."

"Will he hit you again?"

Her laugh sounded very bitter. "Probably."

"Then why go back to him?"

"It's complicated."

"Haven't you got any family?"

"Not around here. Dad's from Essex. I moved down here to be with Luca."

"I'm guessing Luca's got another car beside the Merc?"

She nodded absent-mindedly and dragged on the cigarette again. "Yeah, a Hilux."

"And one of its low beams is faulty, right?"

She looked at me and asked, "How did you know that?"

"Because he's been following us for the last five minutes."

She paled, and her mouth fell open a little. "What did you say?"

I glanced at her and then at the side mirror. "See for yourself."

She turned and looked at the mirror and shook her head. I looked again too. Cruising behind us was Luca's old Hilux, one eye open and one shut down by a blown fuse. She shook her head and gripped the side of the seat with her right hand until the knuckles turned white.

"This can't be happening to me."

"It's not happening to you," I said calmly. "It's happening to us."

"No difference. He's going to go insane when he finds out about the car."

"I don't blame him. Think of the hike in his insurance premiums."

The joke didn't work, and she looked like she was going to be sick.

"I don't know what to do. And just how the hell did he find me?"

"Just stay calm."

The Hilux accelerated without warning and pulled out to overtake us. We were driving south of Lambeth now and crossing into the sprawling Brandon estates. Local authority housing complexes and graffitied tower blocks began to engulf us. I watched the Hilux's uneven headlights as they swerved out into the other lane and approached us in the night. The driving was erratic and the truck was lurching to the left and right. If Luca wasn't careful, he'd be writing off two cars tonight.

"He's overtaking."

"He'll see me."

"Just take it easy."

The pickup was closer now. I saw it was an early model and when it drew alongside us, I saw the coachwork was badly dented and scratched. "Looks like that truck has had a hard life. I thought you said he was a businessman?"

"I did."

"What line of business?"

She sighed. "He's a drug dealer."

My attention was divided between the pickup truck and what Laura had just told me. "A drug dealer?"

"Yeah, and a dangerous one."

Luca's pickup truck accelerated again and cut in front of us, forcing us to a juddering halt on the side of the road at the bottom of a tower block. The Hilux was further across, halfway up on a grass verge. All dark and quiet. Then the driver's door swung open and a heavy-set man slammed the door hard enough to make the whole truck rock on its suspension. He padded over towards us with a knife in his hand.

NINE

The night was full-dark now and our headlights lit iron gates at the base of the tower block's stairwell, just ahead of us to our right. I pushed open the door as Luca drew closer. "Stay in here."

"You can't be thinking of going out there?"

"Why not?"

"You don't know what he's like…"

"I'm about to find out."

I closed the door and turned to face the big man. Then, I heard another door click and turned to see Laura getting out of the Defender. I was angry she had ignored my advice and got out of the vehicle. It would have been a lot easier to handle Luca if she had stayed inside. This way, she could get sucked into things. She walked over and stood beside me.

"What the hell's going on?" he asked.

Now Laura took a step back. "Just take it easy, Luca."

"Who is this bastard and where is my car?"

"I said take it easy. I can explain."

I stepped forward and moved in front of Laura. Luca was a big lad and he knew it. It looked like a good few years of working out in the gym had beefed up his upper body and made him strong. He was wearing a black fleece and the sleeves were stretched tight around his thick arms. The scars on his knuckles told a story, too. He walked over to us with a swagger until he was a foot away and got right up in my face.

"Get out of my way."

I stayed fast. "Get inside the Defender, Laura."

"Who the hell are you, telling my woman what to do?" His Romanian accent was thick.

"I ain't your woman, Luca," Laura called out as she climbed into the vehicle and closed the door.

The young man was getting angry. Laura had defied him to my face, a perfect stranger, and he didn't like it. Blood was rushing to his cheeks, and I felt my right hand curl into a fist. When he leaned closer to me, almost nose to nose, I knew what had to happen next.

"I said, get out of my way!" He pushed into me with his left shoulder as he headed over to Laura in the Defender. "And you, get out of that car now! We're going home."

"Go home, Luca," I said.

He turned, slowly like a bear. I moved fast, bringing my left hand up to block the anticipated strike from his knife-wielding hand while simultaneously driving a jab of my own up into his lower left jaw. The impact of the blow snapped his head back and knocked him off his balance. I followed the strike with another blow to his stomach, aiming right through the wall of muscle and out the other side. The fist powered in hard, landing with a meaty thud in his muscle-packed midriff and punching the air out of his lungs and forcing him to double over and gasp for air.

52

I considered finishing the job by driving my right knee up into his face but rejected it when I thought about Laura watching from back in the Land Rover. Out of nowhere, the heavens opened and a cold rain began to pour down on us once again.

"Get in your truck, and leave."

Laura wound her window down. "That's enough, Blake. He's had enough."

"I said get in your truck and leave, now."

The low hum of the Hilux's engine ticking over filled the tense silence. Its one good low beam was lighting up the surface of the wet street, skimming across it and climbing up the graffitied wall of the tower block. Someone opened a window and asked what was going on. We had been here too long. We were drawing attention to ourselves.

"Now."

Luca straightened up and stared at me, blood running down over his chin from his newly split and swollen lip. The young man had bitten through the lip when I struck his jaw, and he didn't look too happy about it. His eyes were narrow slits of barely concealed rage, but he'd taken a beating and now he got to his feet and took a step back, raising his hand and pointing at me with a meaty, bloody forefinger.

"You're dead, man."

"On your way, now."

"Did you hear what I said? You're dead. I got your number plate, and I know your name. You're dead." He pointed over at the car. "And you too, you bitch! Dead."

I said nothing and didn't move an inch. I watched Luca pad over to the Hilux, climb inside the cab and rev up the engine. He made a big show of reversing off the verge, spitting mud and gravel chips up in two tight arcs before flooring the accelerator and taking off up the road. He screeched around a bend on the estate and moved out of sight.

I turned and walked back to the car. "He's not very polite."

"I'm sorry for all this."

"You have nothing to be sorry about."

"I do. I've got you into trouble. He's not bullshitting, Blake. He means what he says. He's a dangerous man with a lot of close connections to some very nasty people. You said this car was stolen, right?"

"Uh-huh."

"At least he can't trace the number plate." She went quiet and fiddled with her phone. "But how did he find me?"

"Maybe he got lucky," I said. "There's not a lot of traffic around. Or maybe he's tracking your phone."

She gasped. "You can't be serious?"

"We can talk about it later. He's not coming near us again for a while, but we still have to get out of here. Someone around here must have called the cops by now."

"Where?"

I opened the Defender's door. "I saw a construction site back a mile or so."

"A construction site?"

54

I shrugged. "I can't check into a hotel or anywhere else with internal security cameras."

"Why not?"

"Because some people even less pleasant than Luca are hunting me down."

"Why?"

"We can talk about it later. But for now, we have to go. The people hunting me have access to every CCTV camera in the city and facial rec software you think exists only in science fiction films."

"But a construction site?"

"It's our best bet right now. Looks like we're both running away from people and it'll get us out of this rain."

TEN

I drove around the site and checked for cameras. There were four pointing in the usual places and a portacabin at the main entrance. A security guard was inside, asleep with an open magazine resting on his chest. We pulled around to the back of the site. I got out of the battered Defender and pulled open two panels of construction fencing. Then, I returned to the vehicle and we parked up behind a cement mixer truck and killed the engine.

I pulled my tactical vest out of the front footwell and we climbed up a flight of bare concrete steps, making our new home in what would one day be some kind of manager's corner office. The walls were grey cinder blocks and a pallet of electric wiring was stacked up in the corner beside some breeze blocks and tools and steel poles and a dusty nail gun. A light waterproof membrane rigged up on the scaffolding outside kept the wind and rain out.

Laura pulled out her phone and sighed. "What the hell just happened tonight?"

"I'm going to need to take a look at that phone in a minute. It's probably how Luca tracked you down back there."

"I still can't believe it. I knew he was controlling, but tracking me on my phone? My life is such a mess."

I hung the tactical vest over the corner of the pallet and watched the passing traffic through a split in the membrane. Going back through my past, I was also trying to make sense of what had happened and find some sort of explanation. If someone from my past was doing this to me, I sure as hell didn't know who it was. I had made too many enemies. They were strewn across my memories like spent bullet cases rolling away from a gun fight.

After a few seconds, I had it narrowed down to three events that had scarred my life.

The fatal gunfight on Berlin's Nürnberger Straße during a compromised dead drop that had cost the life of an innocent civilian. The night I shot and killed a Russian agent in Moscow when I was escorting a defector out of the country. The look on General Cardoso's face when I helped a rebel group infiltrate and destroy one of his cocaine plantations in Brazil.

People involved with each of these operations had sworn to bring me down, but could it be someone else? Someone closer to me? Someone whose hatred I didn't even know about? Whoever it was, someone was biting back. My head ached with confusion and fatigue. Checking my watch, I saw less than two hours had passed since I had gone on the run and still I had no idea what was going on. Maybe John Grant had some answers, and thanks to Bentinck I knew how to find out.

"Hey," she said quietly. "Penny for your thoughts?"

"Right now they're not even worth that. I just can't work out who could be doing this to me."

"Not pissed off enough people, eh?"

I laughed. "The exact opposite. Hey, you're still bleeding pretty badly."

"It's nothing," she said.

"No, it needs to be patched up. I'll go down to the Defender and get the first aid kit again. Just stay here."

I ran down to the Defender and pulled the first aid kit from the glove box. Scanning the area, I saw there was still no one in sight and I guessed Sleeping Beauty on the other side of the construction site was still enjoying his dreams. As for the three dead men in the back, it was obvious I had to dump it and get a new vehicle. I had killed them in self-defence but if I really was the subject of a set-up, it wouldn't be too hard for whoever was behind it to frame their deaths as another three murders to add to the three dead bodyguards, the Russian woman and Andy Foster back in Connaught Square.

I slammed the door and walked back to the site, pushing through the membrane and running up the cement steps. When I got into the half-built office, I saw Laura standing in the middle of the room. She was holding the gun from my tactical vest in her hands and aiming it at my face.

"Laura? What's going on?"

"Get back!"

I saw only fear in the woman's dark eyes. Glancing down at the business end of the gun, I saw it trembling in her hands. Her right index finger was wrapped around the trigger and she looked even more scared than when she had worked out Luca was behind us in the Hilux.

"Whoa," I said gently. "Take it easy, Laura, and tell me what this is all about."

"You lied to me."

The gun was shaking more now, the muzzle jerking in tiny vertical arcs as she struggled to keep it aimed at me. It was heavier than she had thought it would be. The weapon was an Austrian Glock 17. Just like their American counterparts, there was no safety catch. If her finger moved a fraction of an inch, I was taking a nine mil in the chest.

"I don't know what you're talking about, but you need to lower the gun before someone gets hurt."

"Not someone," she said. "You. You're a liar."

"What is this about?"

She tipped her head towards her phone. It was on top of the pallet. "I saw you on the news when you were out. They say you're a killer. That you murdered someone in the government. They said you're highly dangerous and not to be approached. Now, take back that step you just took towards me when I was talking or I'll shoot you with this thing, I swear."

I made another quick study of her face. Framed by half-wet chestnut brown hair, her eyes were blinking anxiously. Full red lips quivering slightly in the low light of a streetlight shining in through the membrane. She was no killer, but a fatal accident with the gun was possible.

"Whatever they're saying I did, it's not true."

"Why should I believe you? Now I know why you were driving like a maniac across the bridge. You were trying to escape! That's why they're hunting you!"

"Yes, I was trying to escape, but not because I murdered anyone in the government. I don't know why, but I'm being set up."

"Now I've heard it all."

"It's true. I'm in the SAS just like I said I was. Tonight I was on an operation to snatch a foreign agent and bring her to a neutral safehouse for her own safety. Or that's what I thought I was doing. When I got to the target's address everything went crazy. My men killed everyone in the house, turned on me and told me they were going to kill me. So, I went on the run."

She lowered the gun. It was still shaking. "You could say anything. I don't trust you."

"I saved your life. I could have left you in the car to drown and instead I risked my own life to pull you out. I protected you from Luca. Do they sound like the actions of someone you need to fear?"

She sighed and dropped the gun down to her side.

"Put the gun on the floor, Laura. Put it on the floor and step away from it."

She was still unsure. I watched her think it over. Then, she did as I had asked. I walked slowly over to the gun, clicked the mag out of the grip and put both the weapon and the ammunition back in my tactical vest. Then I walked over to her in the middle of the room.

"You did the right thing," I said. "I am not going to harm you, I promise."

"But *I* will."

I recognised the Romanian accent instantly from back on the side of the road in the housing estate. I guessed my theory about the phone tracker was right after all, but it was still hard to believe he had come back for more so soon.

"Step away from my woman, stranger."

I looked up and saw Laura's face first. She was staring at Luca, her face ashen with terror. When I turned to face him, the big Romanian was standing in the doorway to the office with a chipped, scratched pistol stuffed into his waistband and a wide grin on his face.

"I said you were a dead man," he said, reaching for the gun. "And I meant it."

ELEVEN

I knew what was coming next. You see it in their eyes, a wild flash of confidence and power. The gun I had just taken from Laura was still in the inside pocket of my tactical vest currently hanging over the corner of the pallet on the other side of the room. It was a stupid mistake. When he pulled the ageing Makarov pistol from his waistband and pointed it at my face, I knew just how stupid.

"What is this, Laura?" he asked. "I'm confused. Where is my car? Were you trying to steal it from me? Tell me before I kill this man."

She took a step back, shocked into silence by his arrival on the construction site. I calculated that the nail gun was the closest weapon, but still too far to reach without taking a bullet first. If his gun was even loaded.

"How the hell are you even here, Luca?" Laura asked.

"You don't ask me questions, bitch. I ask the questions. Who is this man?"

He waved the gun casually in my face and then aimed it at her. Truth was, Luca Antonescu was starting to irritate me. I was in the middle of a major storm involving several murders and by now a nationwide manhunt with me as the target. The last thing I needed was to get involved with a low-level woman-beating, drug-dealing scumbag like him but my conscience wouldn't let me abandon Laura.

She swallowed her fear and answered his question with a quiet, trembling voice. I guessed she had seen too many of his tempers and knew what he was capable of. She was frightened about what he was going to do not only to her but to me, the guy on the street sucked into her car crash of a life.

"He's no one. He helped me," she said meekly.

His brow furrowed and he cocked his head to one side as if he had misheard her. "Helped you?"

"I nearly died. Listen, how did you find me tonight? When I left the house you were talking to Stoica on the phone. You had no way of knowing where I was."

He hesitated. Glanced at the phone in her hands.

She gasped. "You really are tracking my phone!"

Silence.

"You're spying on me!"

He was getting angry. "Can you blame me? I let a bitch like you out of my sight for one second and you steal my car and meet up with someone I don't even know."

"I didn't steal your car. I just took it because I was angry. It crashed into the river."

"It did what?"

"Take it easy, Luca," I said.

He looked at me with a snarl on his lips. "I didn't tell you to speak. You don't speak unless I tell you. Get your hands up in the air where I can see them nice and clear and step away from the nail gun."

So he had seen it, too. Luca wasn't as stupid as I had thought. I obeyed, raised my hands and stepped away from the nail gun. Laura was shivering, maybe cold, maybe fear, maybe both.

"Big man – you stay there and be quiet," Luca said. "Laura, you get over here and stand behind me."

As she walked over the concrete to Luca, I kept my eyes on the barrel of the gun in his hand.

"Say goodbye to your friend, Laura, and get into my truck."

She turned to go. "What about him?"

"Never mind about him, just do as you are told before I get even angrier than I already am."

I was still too far away to disarm him, and now nowhere near the nail gun.

As he moved closer for the kill, Laura and I caught each other's eye and when she winked at me from behind his back I knew what she was thinking. Instead of leaving the room, she reached down and picked up a length of metal piping beside the pallet of plastic cables. She was taking a big risk standing up to him. He was bigger and stronger than her and if she got it wrong or lost her nerve he'd probably kill us both.

She needed my help. A distraction. "You kill unarmed men a lot?"

"Only when they beg for it. As you are about to do."

She had the pipe in her hands now and was straightening up to her full height.

"You seem like a nice guy."

"If you think I'm bad, you should meet my brother Stoica. Isn't that right, Laura?"

He had raised his voice to reach her on her way to the door, and now he turned to see if she had left the room. Instead, he saw her standing behind him with the pipe. This was a problem.

"What the hell?" he said, swivelling around and pointing the gun at her.

I acted fast, running to the nail gun and turning it on. I had used these on construction sites in Thailand when I was a younger man, and I knew they had a speed of around one hundred feet per second and a maximum range of fifty yards. Luca was much less than half that distance and when I fired the first nail, it split the shin bone on his left leg in two, decking him in a heartbeat.

"Get behind the pallet!" I yelled.

Laura dived down behind the massive pallet of cabling as Luca screamed in pain and returned fire, half emptying the magazine wildly in my direction. It was a foolish and rash thing to do, but I understood it and I expected it. I was already behind the stack of breeze blocks in a solid defensive position, but too far from Laura to help her to safety out of the room.

"Let her go, Luca," I called out. "Throw your gun down and let her leave."

"I will kill you both, you dogs!"

I had no more words for Luca. I leaned slowly around the edge of the breeze blocks and fired the nail gun a second time, driving a four-inch nail through his left forearm. "Next one goes in your head."

"All right," he screamed, hoarse now. "Okay. Go. Take the bitch. She's nothing."

"Gun down, Luca. Slide it over to me."

He obeyed, dropping the Makarov into the dust and sloppily spinning over in my direction. I switched off the nail gun, threw it into the far corner of the room and walked over to the pistol. "You did the right thing, Luca."

"Die, you dog."

I checked the mag and saw he had three rounds left. Pocketed the mag and the pistol and then walked over to my tactical vest. I put it on and drew my Glock. "It's safe to come out now, Laura."

Slowly, she appeared from behind the pallet, her hands gently trembling. "Is he going to be all right?"

"Call an ambulance," I said. "And then disable your Wi-Fi and sign out of Google. That's how he's tracking you." I turned to Luca. "We're off now, son. Your ride will be here in a minute. Bother me again and I'll finish you off, got it?"

"Big words from a man with a gun threatening an unarmed man."

I put my gun back inside my vest. "That arrangement didn't seem to bother you when it was the other way around."

Before he replied, I drove a powerful jab into his face and knocked him out cold. His head smacked back on the concrete floor and Laura gasped.

"Was that necessary?"

"Let's get out of here. I have business to do."

She turned and looked at the unconscious man with wide eyes. "What sort of business?"

"Saving my life."

"I don't understand. Is it really that bad?"

"Never mind. We have to lose the Defender, too. It has a nasty surprise in the back we don't want to get caught with. I saw an old Jaguar on the road just past the site. C'mon."

"Have you got the keys for it?"

"More or less."

"What does that even mean?"

"You'll find out."

"Why not just take the Hilux?"

"First, because they'll report it stolen and give our ID to the police. The owner of the car we're about to steal has no idea who took it. Second, it has a faulty headlight that might attract some bored cops. We don't need any of that tonight."

I picked up a chunk of rubble and she followed me off the site. As we walked, she called an ambulance out. Then we reached the Jag. I had chosen it because it was an eighties model and, despite the rudimentary central locking system, that meant less security. I put the rubble through the driver's window, pulled up the lock pin, brushed the broken glass off the seat and climbed inside. Then I leant over and opened the passenger door. "Get in."

She got in out of the rain and I was already removing the small vinyl cover guard beneath the steering column.

"What are you doing?"

"Looking for something."

"For what?"

"A wiring harness connector."

I located the loose coil of electrical wires and started to tease them apart. This was where the wires to the ignition, starter and battery were located. I pulled a commando dagger from the inverted holster on my tactical vest and stripped back the insulation on the battery wires and carefully twisted the copper strands together with my thumb and forefinger. Having ensured a good flow of electricity to the ignition when I turned the starter, I now joined the ignition and battery wires together. The dash lights flickered to life and lit our faces a warm amber.

"Almost there."

"What if Luca wakes up?"

"Forget about him. He's not going anywhere until he's been to a hospital." I sparked the wires and the engine turned over. "And we're out of here."

TWELVE

We drove to meet Wainwright in silence. Bentinck had told me Grant's code: Arthur on 1 March. Meaningless to most people but not to me. Arthur was a reference to John Grant's old haunt, a nightclub called Camelot, and 1 March simply meant 0200 hours. Each month was divided into two to make twenty-four and these twenty-four indicated which hour. First half of January was 0000 hours to 0030 hours. Second half 0030 hours to 0100 hours. So, any date in the first half of March meant 0200. It worked for us. Two a.m. at the Camelot nightclub.

As we drove, I was thinking about what Bentinck had told me about John Grant being on the run. Beside me, Laura was probably thinking about Luca and what had gone down back at the construction site. No matter. We didn't know each other well enough for the silence to be awkward and the hotwired Jaguar was faster and smoother than the wrecked Defender, despite the smashed front window. We made good time across the city. Luckily, she never asked me about what was in the back of the Land Rover.

I pulled into the car park and we climbed out into the cold night. "This shouldn't take long."

"Should I stay in the car?" she asked.

"No, you're safer with me."

With the smashed window, I was unhappy about leaving the tactical vest inside the cab so I walked around and threw it in the boot. That was when I noticed a small portable tyre repair kit and jack. I considered taking the jack handle into the club as a defensive weapon but tossed the idea out. Getting caught at the door with something like that meant trouble and maybe even police. I settled for moving the jack handle, a good sturdy piece of iron, under the front seat for easier access just in case and then we walked over to the busy, bright club. Light spilt out onto the wet tarmac and reflected in the puddles outside the door. A bass beat thumped in the night. There was no queue. Inside, I scanned the ground floor and found an empty table with a good view of all the doors. I told Laura to grab it for us while I got some drinks up at the bar.

Back at the table, we chinked the two beer bottles and tried to look like it was just another night for a regular couple. It was a modern club built into a former factory with red brick walls and painted arches. Expensive tapered drum shades hung from the ceiling and a second tier of seating was situated on a mezzanine balcony to the right of the bar.

We took a seat and sipped our drinks. We waited thirty minutes before Wainwright entered. He was late and I wondered why but I clocked him as soon as he walked in. He was a small, wiry individual in a black pea coat and grey scarf and he wandered over to a fruit machine near the door. After a few seconds had passed, he turned and walked over to our table. As I reached for my bottle, he slid in next to Laura.

"I'm Wainwright. Take it easy with the glass bottle."

"I don't do easy." I watched a man leaning against the bar, drinking. He had been staring at Laura since we walked in.

Wainwright nodded. "Glad you could make it, Colonel."

"I'd rather be anywhere else."

"Who's the girl?"

Laura looked at him sharply. "I'm right here. Don't talk about me like I'm not right here."

"She's a friend," I said.

She sipped her beer. "Actually, we just met."

Wainwright's eyes searched my face. "Are you crazy? She could be anyone."

"I'm not anyone, I'm someone. And I'm still right here."

I said, "Given the circumstances of how we met, I'd say I can trust her. Now drop it."

Wainwright shrugged and cleared his throat. "As you wish."

"What have you got for me?" I asked.

"You need to speak with Grant."

"I already know that."

"But you can't get in touch."

"No."

"Since your raid went south, Bentinck was ordered to shut down the entire department tighter than a camel's arse in a sandstorm."

"I got that, too. Can he be trusted?"

"Who, Mike Bentinck? He's an old blue from Christ's Hospital."

"But can he be trusted?"

"I just said so, didn't I?"

I wasn't reassured. "Tell me you have a way of contacting Grant. Make me happy."

"You're in luck." He reached into his coat pocket and I gripped the bottle again. The music over on the dancefloor seemed to get louder. "Relax, Blake – I'm just getting you the number. You don't need to smash a bottle and stab me with it."

"Just get on with it."

He handed me a slip of paper. "Here."

I checked the paper and saw a standard British mobile number. "Thanks."

"More than welcome." He moved to go, pushing the chair back and getting to his feet. Then, he tightened his scarf and put his hands in his pockets. "This meeting never happened."

I watched Wainwright leave the pub and disappear into the rainy night. The paper he had given me contained what I hoped was the number of a burner phone belonging to Grant. I just hoped he was still alive enough to answer it and talk to me.

"What now?" Laura asked.

"Now, we go back to the car and call Grant."

"I need to call my dad, first."

We went outside. I told her to use the car for the call and I went for a walk around the club. She seemed cagey about it and I didn't know why. I gave her five minutes and then grew suspicious. I wasn't worried about Luca – by now he would be in an Accident and Emergency Department trying to explain how he'd been shot twice with an industrial nail gun, but something felt wrong so I decided to go back to the Jag. When I got to the car, there was no sign of her so I scanned the car park. At first, I saw nothing but then heard a scuffle and a woman's gasp from behind what looked like the club's toilets. I walked over and saw Laura trying to fight off the oily charmer who had given her the eye in the club. Now he was trying it on with her. Then he got tasty, pinned her up in the corner behind two giant commercial waste bins and drew a flick knife from his pocket.

THIRTEEN

I pulled my roll neck up against the wind and made my way over to them. The fear on her face faded when she saw me approaching. Then, the guy with the knife turned and snarled at me and told me to get lost. I didn't have time for this.

"Laura, get in the car."

"She ain't going nowhere."

I stepped closer. I was unarmed but he was drunk. In the half-hour we were waiting for Wainwright inside the pub, I'd watched him down two pints of beer and four single whiskies. That made him more dangerous but less capable.

"You stop talking," I said. "Laura, get into the Jag."

He turned now, putting himself between me and Laura and then raising the knife in my face. "You what, mate?"

"No more words from you." I saw his shoulder twitch inside his fake leather jacket. This told me he was about to move his arm a fraction of a second later. I did two things. I brought my hand up in front of my body and smacked him hard on the inside of his wrist with my knuckles and knocked the knife from his hand. As it clattered on the wet tarmac I did the second thing and launched a premier league headbutt into the centre of his face. His nose crumbled like a used airbag and blood burst out across his face. Then I powered a hard jab into the left side of his jaw and sent him down to the ground like a felled oak.

Laura screamed and brought her hands up to her face. "Is he dead?"

"No, he's just an arsehole. Let's get out of here."

She stared down at him. The rain was washing the blood off his face and streaming down onto the ground around his head. "Should we call an ambulance?"

"Laura, he was trying to rob you, or a hell of a lot worse. Let him lie there till he wakes up. He looked like he could do with a shower anyway. He's just a greasy toerag."

"I don't know…"

"Yeah, you do. C'mon."

We walked over to the car and climbed in. Inside the Jag, I switched the phone on speaker and put it on the dashboard. After Laura's earlier comment about how she didn't feel she could trust me, it was the best I could come up with. Then I heard the voice of my old friend.

"All good, John?" I asked.

"Are you alone, Bill?"

I turned to Laura and put my finger on my lips before replying, "Yes."

"Listen, things are going pear-shaped in a big way, old man. There's a ton of shit flying around and a lot of it is coming in your direction."

"What's going on, John? I need to know."

A long, steady pause. I heard the metallic clicking of his cigar lighter. "Operation Wildhorse."

I paused and felt my skin prickling up my arms and neck. Anything given a formal, operational codename usually meant senior sanction and a lot of trouble. "Not heard of Wildhorse, John. Is this a D19 operation?"

"No more on the phone, Bill. I've already said too much. Good to know you're still alive, by the way."

"Same goes for you. How long have you had the burner phone?" I asked.

"A few hours. Enough time for it to have been compromised."

"Tapping can only move that fast if it's sanctioned by the very top, John. What the hell is this all about?"

"Not now. You're an old operator, Bill. You know the deal."

Operator. Not a word I used very often myself, it described a member of the SAS. "We're all old operators, John. Why am I the one being chased into a fox covert with the hounds at full cry?"

"Meet me tomorrow when I'll have more information for you."

"What sort of information?"

"Information that could save your life."

"Where and when?"

"South side of St James's Park. Six AM. I'll be on the bench."

The call ended. Laura said, "If this is so important, why can't he meet you now? I mean, why wait until morning?"

"There could be any number of reasons why. He could have flipped and he's setting a trap to catch me. Maybe he thinks I'm doing the same thing and he wants time to get some protection. Maybe he's hiding evidence. Maybe he's afraid of the dark. Either way, we're not meeting him until tomorrow morning."

"And what did he mean when he said Wildhorse?"

"That's a very good question. It sounds like some kind of intelligence or military operation but after that, I'm in the dark."

"So what do we do in the meantime? I can't go back to my place. Luca will have someone watching it."

"I know a place, belongs to a mate of mine. He's overseas right now, on a job. We can stay there for the night and then meet Grant after breakfast."

"You have a key to this place?"

"More or less."

*

Matt Huntshaw's flat was in Pimlico, a small well-heeled area of London full of Regency townhouses and neatly manicured garden squares. Houses here were priced in the millions, but Matt's place was a more modest basement flat ten minutes' walk from the underground station. I parked the car in Matt's space and we walked back to the flat. When we got there, I opened the wrought iron gate, went down the steps and reached his door. I already knew the lock was a straight-forward pin tumbler over forty years old and wouldn't keep us out in the wet and cold for long.

I reached into a pocket on my tactical vest and pulled out a small tool pouch and opened it up.

"What's that?" she asked.

"My key."

I selected a small rake and tensioner spanner and carefully slotted the spanner into the bottom end of the keyhole. Then I gently pulled back on the spanner to apply the correct pressure inside the lock and pushed in the rake above it. Sliding the rake back and forth, I was able to line up the tiny gap between the key pins and the driver pins and line them up with the shear line. As soon as I felt they were aligned I extracted the spanner and pushed the door open.

"Et voilà."

"I thought you said he was a friend?" Laura said. "I thought you said you had a key?"

"I said he was a mate, and I said I had a key *more or less*."

"A lock pick is a bit on the *less* side, don't you think?"

I shrugged and pushed the door open. "In you go. Safe in here for the night."

"This is breaking and entering."

"Matty would never press charges. I saved his life in Afghanistan."

"It's still against the law."

I dangled the car keys up in her face. "Here. Sleep in the Jag. Nice soft leather seats and one smashed window that lets in the rain. I'll walk around after breakfast."

She brushed past me without saying a word and I closed the door behind us, pushing the bolt across. In the kitchen, I set about going through Matt's cupboards until I found a jar of instant coffee and I made two cups. No milk. When I got into the sitting room, Laura was holding another pistol, a vintage World War II-era British officer's Webley.

"Don't worry," I said. "It's not dangerous. Matt removed the firing pin. It's the law."

She turned the old handgun over in her hands, studying it for a few seconds.

"When you said this Matt guy was abroad on a job, what sort of work is that?"

"This and that."

"You mean he kills people?"

"Not specifically, no, although it might be required from time to time."

She was quiet for a long time, then she set the heavy Webley back down on the shelf. She turned and flopped down on his armchair. She looked exhausted, and so was I.

"Here, have a coffee – it's been a long day."

She peered inside.

"Sorry, no milk. It's black or nothing."

. She sipped it. "Too hot."

"You're welcome."

"Sorry."

I set the cup down on a side table and crashed down on the couch. "Yeah, long day."

After another of her long silences, she said, "Why are these people doing this to you, Bill?"

It was a good question. Since the raid back at the Russian safehouse, my life had been a series of rapid-fire explosions, detonated in quick succession and giving me no time to think. The only clue I had was John Grant's reference to Operation Wildhorse, but without further information that meant practically nothing. I had never heard the word before and I had no idea what sort of operation it related to or who was running it. Recalling Gilmore's comment about what was happening tonight and how it affected national security, it wasn't a great leap to see that this Wildhorse was going to lead down a pretty deep and unpleasant rabbit hole.

"I don't know," I said, "but I'm not going to stop until I find out."

"You're very persistent."

"It's sort of a basic requirement in my line of work."

"Does your friend smoke?"

I pointed above her head. "You're sitting in his favourite chair, so what do you think?"

She looked up and saw a nicotine-yellow bloom staining the ceiling white. Without another word, she pulled her cigarettes out and lit one. Then tossed one over to me. I caught it and then her lighter which she threw over a second later. Then she blew out a long column of blue smoke and sank into the armchair. "That is better."

"Yeah."

Another long drag. "Where are you from, Bill?"

"Originally?"

"Yes."

"Family are from Oxford and London. Nowhere and nothing special."

"Rich family?"

"Not particularly."

"Did you go to university at Oxford?"

"No. I went to college outside the city and then straight to Sandhurst."

She looked at me, confused.

"It's the training college for army officers."

She flicked some ash in the ashtray Matt kept balanced on the arm of his chair. "What then?"

"The Parachute Regiment was my first choice at selection and I was lucky enough to get in. It's not easy and neither should it be. After that, I applied to get into the Special Air Service and eventually with a lot of hard work I made that happen. It's not what people think it is, but it was a good fit for me."

"You did something with your life. You must be proud."

"Maybe. You look tired. You should get some sleep."

She paused. "There's only one bedroom in this flat, right?"

"And it's yours. I'll sleep on this couch."

She stubbed out her cigarette and got up from the chair. "Goodnight, Bill."

FOURTEEN

When Laura surfaced the next morning and started making coffee, I went into Matt's bedroom. A tactical ops jacket is not the best thing to wear when you're trying to keep a low profile, and I was still wearing my original black trousers and tactical riot boots from the raid, too. Matt was roughly the same size as me, so I quickly grabbed a pair of clean jeans and a shirt and then helped myself to the leather barn coat he'd bought on a trip to the US a few years back.

Kitted up in the new gear, I splashed some water on my face and drank the coffee with Laura. Then the two of us went to the car in Matt's parking space and drove north. A mist had settled over the city in the night and we inched forward in heavier traffic, mostly saying nothing. This was just as well – my mind was still on overdrive trying to figure out what was going on. I still had nothing – just a fleeting, casual reference to national security and the name of a classified operation: Wildhorse. It was something but it wasn't enough.

Across my career in the regular SAS and then in D19, I had been involved in a lot of classified operations. Some of these were abroad. I had worked alongside British SIS agents on missions in Afghanistan, Pakistan, Iraq, Iran, Syria,

Hong Kong and several west African countries. We also operated at home. Northern Ireland, Manchester, London.

These were top secret jobs that don't get talked about. Dangerous, difficult and sometimes depressing. They required a great deal of planning and often involved complicated logistics. Knowledge was compartmentalised. Whatever Wildhorse was, no one in D19 seemed to know anything about it. That alone made it very interesting. D19 was a very well connected division at the heart of the SAS with close contacts in the intel sector. And despite no one in D19 knowing about it, we seemed to be its targets. The pressure was on to dig to the bottom of the barrel and find out who was trying to take us down.

We pulled up and parked on a side street. Double yellow lines, residents' parking only, meters, cameras and all the other things that make driving in London such a pleasure. None of it mattered today, so I just cut the engine and we walked away from the car. If we got back and found it had been clamped or towed or reported stolen and taken away by the police, I'd just have to borrow another one from somewhere else. Given what I was up against, car theft was not going to add much to a prison sentence for at least eight murders.

Grant was sitting on a bench in St James's Park under an umbrella in the rain. He was sitting perfectly still and staring out across the lake. At first, he was just a silhouette in the misty gloom, wearing a long black trench coat and holding the umbrella. For a second, it crossed my mind he was already dead. I turned and looked over my shoulder to see if we were being followed. Scanned the horizon for any sign of unwanted company.

We pushed on. It was six o'clock and the park had been open an hour. On our way to meet him, Laura and I had grabbed some food at the Shell petrol station in Southwark and driven through Waterloo, crossing the river on Westminster Bridge. I dumped the car at the eastern end of Birdcage Walk and the two of us walked through the deserted park in the low pre-dawn light. We were less than a mile from Hyde Park where I fled from the box trucks and it wasn't good to be back.

As we walked, I looked over my shoulder to make sure we had no unwanted friends, but we were alone. I felt my heart speed up in my chest as the meeting with Grant drew closer. Laura shivered and slipped her hand through my arm.

"It's cold."

"Yeah," I said.

"Is that him up ahead?" she asked.

"That's him."

I scanned the immediate vicinity for any signs of trouble. I saw no one except a single man jogging along the shore. We walked around the far end of the lake to the north shore. "You stay here," I said. "Keep your eyes open and if you see anything that looks like funny business call my mobile."

"Funny business?"

"Anyone out of place. Anyone paying too much attention to me and Grant. And keep an eye on that bloke jogging around the lake."

"Am I in danger?"

"I wouldn't have thought so. I only met you a few hours ago and no one knows who you are."

I left Laura behind and walked around the lake to Grant, approaching him from the side and then pulling up to a stop beside him, hands in my pockets. I watched some ducks on the smooth surface of the water.

"John."

"Bill," he said quietly. "Nice of you to join me."

"I'm hoping for your sake there isn't going to be any unpleasantness here this morning. I trust you, John. That trust is not going to get broken, is it?"

Grant shook his head and rubbed his nose with a leather-gloved finger. When he spoke, his breath plumed out into the air a foot in front of his face. "How far do we go back, Bill?"

"Maybe a little too far."

He gave a hoarse chuckle. "Perhaps you're right."

A long pause as I tracked the jogger. He was running towards us now. I knew he was unarmed from when I had seen him earlier. His arms were at his sides, bent at the elbow in the usual way people hold them when running. He wore normal running clothes and had little white earbuds in his ears. Probably music, I thought. Or the voice of whoever was controlling him. As he approached, I reached into my pocket and grabbed hold of my keys, carefully pushing some of the bigger ones through the gaps in my knuckles with my right thumb. It wasn't the first time I'd improvised a knuckle-duster this way and wouldn't be the last.

The jogger ran past us without giving any indication he'd even seen us. I could tell from his breathing he was fit and the jog was no effort, not even on this cold morning. I made a note of how long it would be before he got around the lake and was back around where Laura was sitting and then spoke again.

"Why am I here, John?"

"Because you asked to meet me."

"You know what I mean, and don't waste my time. A few hours ago life was normal, or as normal as it gets for me. I was setting out on a regular D19 mission to bring a Russian agent into protective custody and when I get there my own team shoot her dead and try and kill me, too."

"Interesting, isn't it?"

"That's not the word I'd use, John. I'd say something very ugly is going on."

"You'd be right. I have something for you."

He reached his hand inside the top of his trench coat and I pivoted around to face him, hand still gripping the keys.

"Take it easy, Bill. It's just a piece of paper."

"Can't take any chances, John. You know how this game works."

"We're all on edge. Just keep some perspective and remember who your friends are. You need to talk to Peter Brookline. He has the answers you need."

Brookline was a good man. He and I had served together on too many missions to count but he had much loftier ambitions than I had ever harboured. A graduate of Cambridge, he had joined the UOTC – the University

Officers' Training Corp. This is an army reserve unit that is part of the RMA Sandhurst Group. It advises on passing the officers' commissions board. Opens a window in life at Sandhurst as well as introducing young aspiring army officers to weapons and organising visits to regiments. A lot of high-flyers start that way. Brookline and I had spent a lot of time at the depot together during our years in P Company and now I was praying he was still alive.

"I already tried to speak with him. His number has been cut."

"He's on the run, just like you are. Just like we all are. D19 operators are being flushed out and hunted down and taken out."

"Brookline's on the outside? This is crazy. He's as establishment as you get."

"Not anymore. You can contact him here." He leaned over and stretched his arm out, his black-gloved hand holding a piece of crisp folded white paper out to me. I took it.

"This is for you, and don't—"

He stopped talking with a jolt and pulled his hand back to his body, reaching up and gripping his throat. He leaned back on the bench and released his grip on the umbrella, which now tipped back and balanced on his shoulder for a few seconds before toppling over and falling into the wet tarmac behind the bench.

"John?"

His face was turning purple, the colour of rotten plums and his eyes were bulging in their sockets so hard I thought they were about to explode.

"What's happening?" he gasped, white froth building at the corners of his mouth. His body was rigid now, like an ironing board. His great long legs stretched out straight and started violently shaking.

I knew what was happening. We both did.

"Take it easy, old friend."

I scanned the area for any sign of the jogger. He had to have a hand in this somehow. I saw him running west to east along the north shore gradually getting closer to Laura.

"Get out of here!" Grant croaked, imploring me with his crazed, bloodshot eyes to get away to safety, and then he was dead. The tension instantly fell away from his body and he went limp, arms by his sides and legs bent under the bench. His head slumped to the right, his blood-soaked chin coming to rest on his perfectly ironed shirt and silk tie.

I stepped away from the bench and began to run around the eastern end of the lake as I pulled my phone from my pocket and rang Laura.

"Hi. What the hell happened to the man you were talking—"

"Get up from the bench and turn to your left. Make your way to the east end of the lake. Do it now, Laura."

"What's happening?"

"Do as I say. They killed John Grant. They know I was talking to him here and they'll certainly have seen you with me by now. You probably already have a file. You need to meet me at the eastern end of the lake now. I think the man jogging was the assassin."

"They killed him?"

"Do it now!"

I cut the call and sprinted around the lake. I had no idea how they had taken my friend out – I hadn't seen the jogger do anything that looked suspicious. He hadn't sneezed or moved his arms in any strange way to fire something concealed on himself. All I knew was he was making his way closer to Laura and if my suspicions were right he knew who she was and that she was close to me.

I turned around to my left and made my way west along the north shore. Where was she? Bare winter trees scratched the leaden sky above my head as I scanned the mist for any signs of her. Instead, I saw the jogger. He was looming out of the mist, a grey silhouette running fast towards me, his trainers pounding the wet pavement in perfect timing at one-forty beats per minute.

And still no sign of Laura.

Had he already got to her?

Was he just an innocent passer-by?

I turned to my right and headed into the trees, moving away from the jogger. He kept on his route, no deviation as he made his way along the path and then headed towards the eastern exit. I pulled up to a stop against the trunk of a giant oak tree and hit the speed dial. When the phone rang, I heard it just off to my left in the mist. I turned and saw Laura, walking towards me.

"Are you okay?" I asked.

She nodded. "What happened?"

"Not here."

"Can we get back to the car?" she asked with a shiver.

"Yes. We can speak there. This is much worse than I thought."

FIFTEEN

To my surprise, the Jag was still parked up on Birdcage Walk. I'd counted on it getting clocked by the council or police on a CCTV and towed but I guess the mist was slowing them down. We climbed inside and locked the doors. I turned on the engine and fired up the heater. Indicated and pulled out, driving back along the southern edge of the park. I checked the mirror and saw nothing suspicious going on behind us, but after what had just happened I was on edge. It was starting to feel like the entire machinery of the British state was gearing up to crush me.

"I saw him coming," she said, warming her hands in front of the plastic heating vent. "When I was talking to you on the phone and you said that maybe had something to do with the jogger. He was pretty far away so I got up and headed into the trees near the café. I guessed he'd find it much harder to track me down over there."

"You did the right thing. I'm sorry I put you in danger."

She shrugged. "I'm fine. What happened to the man you were talking to? It was hard to see clearly in the mist but I saw him collapse and struggle."

"He died. I think it was some sort of nerve agent but I can't work out how they got him."

"I've never seen anything like that before in my whole life. It was terrible."

"You shouldn't have had to see it," I said. "And that's why we're parting company. I need to take you somewhere that's safe, somewhere you can stay until all this blows over."

"There's no need. It's the most exciting thing that's ever happened to me."

"It's not a game, Laura. Where can I take you that's safe?"

She went quiet, pushing back into the Jag's soft seat and enjoying the warmth. More relaxed now, her head rolled on the headrest as I took a right and turned north onto Spur Road, cruising past Buckingham Palace and heading across the roundabout onto Constitution Hill.

"Fine," she said at last. "My Dad's place."

"Is it safe?"

"Yes."

"And where is it?"

"Near Harlow."

"Essex?"

"Yeah," she said. "He runs a haulage company from there, driving stuff in from Europe. Is that too far?"

I turned right and headed into Mayfair. "It's no problem at all. We can be there in less than three hours." I checked the clock on the dash. "Just in time for a late breakfast."

"Listen, when I told you about Luca I kept something back."

Checked the mirror, changed up a gear and weaved around a car trundling along in the slow lane. "What?"

"It's about the drugs."

"I'm listening."

"He deals the drugs with his brother, a man called Stoica. They work for a man named Sorin. The drugs come in from Europe on trucks."

"I think I see where this is going. Your father."

"He doesn't want to do it, Blake. They're forcing him to do it. They say if he doesn't let them bring the drugs into the country inside his fleet, they'll kill me. They have us locked down, trapped in a corner."

"Bad."

"Dad doesn't know what to do. He hates his life since Luca reeled me in. He talks all the time about selling up and running away but I don't think he'll ever do it. He's scared they'll catch up with us and hurt me, or worse."

"Tell me more about the drug-running operation."

"It's simple enough. Dad's company isn't big enough to draw too much attention to itself, but he has enough lorries to ensure a constant flow of drugs into the country. The drugs are loaded into secret compartments under the flooring of the containers, usually in Holland or France and then onto ferries. They use Dad because he runs mostly refrigerated containers and that means they can't find the drugs with thermal imaging equipment."

"Which ports does he come into?"

"Depends on the pickup location but usually Folkestone or Lowestoft."

"What do you know about this Sorin guy?"

"Not much. I've never even met him. I think he has a place in the West End. I know he drives a big black car.

Brand new, and Luca and Stoica seem pretty scared of him. If the deliveries are held up for any reason at customs or the ferry crossings are cancelled because of bad weather, it's Sorin this and Sorin that."

"Sounds like a real charmer. Listen, why don't you get some sleep and I'll wake you when we're there."

No response.

I turned and looked at her, and she was already asleep. Bringing her with me to St. James's Park had been a stupid mistake. She could have been taken hostage and used to smoke me out. She could have been killed. Now, she was probably already the subject of a comprehensive MI5 file somewhere. She had me to thank for that.

The windscreen wipers swept back and forth hypnotically as I fought through the traffic. Changing lanes, stopping for lights, mirrors, overtaking, sliding back into the slow lane. Half a million CCTV cameras in this city. Outside of communist China, more than anywhere else in the world per capita. Each one swivelling and spying and monitoring people as they went about their business. The government reassured people these were on every street corner and building to fight crime, but with crime levels ever higher each year, this excuse would run out of steam sooner or later.

The cameras were there for exactly the same reason they were in totalitarian China – as part of an extensive surveillance network to monitor not criminals but the general population. Today, there would be several teams of people working around the clock to track me down and follow me wherever I wanted to go. They would be backed up by the same satellite tracking they had used to catch me the first time.

We had used this latest generation of spy satellites a lot in D19. These weren't optical satellites so they could be used to see through any kind of weather including heavy cloud cover. These reconnaissance satellites can see anyone, anywhere, at any time and the only problem they present is how expensive they are to run. Once sanctioned by the right authority, a team can forget about the cost and just track someone.

Today, that someone was me, but they had to find me first. I would change cars soon. Get out of the city and try and lose all the tails they were trying to pin on me. My priority was to get Laura out of the line of fire. Sooner or later, she was going to get hurt or killed and that would be on me.

I cruised north in moderate traffic through Holloway, Haringey and Wood Green. I knew the area well from years before and was shocked by how much it had changed. I was expecting deterioration but it was the opposite. New shopping centres and young, planted trees on the pavements. Fresh tarmac on the roads made for a smooth ride.

I thought about what Laura had told me about the drugs. It made sense. She was sullen and subdued but I could see she was a good person. That's why Luca didn't make sense. Now, all the pieces fell into place. He and his brother Stoica had been ordered to reel her in so they could trap and blackmail her father into running the drugs. Her father had the capacity to bring industrial quantities through the ports and if he tried to back out they would kill his daughter. Maybe it was a bluff, but I wouldn't count on it, and neither had her father.

It was an impossible situation for him. There was no going to the law. Men like Sorin have long memories and bad tempers. They never forgive or forget and their bloodlust is insatiable. All this meant more problems. I couldn't leave Laura and her dad at the mercy of Sorin and his men, but at the same time, I had bigger fish to fry in the shape of Wildhorse.

Then I saw it again.

When I checked the mirror to turn right and head into Walthamstow there it was, a brand new black Mercedes-Benz S-Class. A great big beast of a car with smooth, aquiline lines and headlights like panther's eyes. It had been two or three cars back since Stoke Newington and I'd thought nothing of it, but now we were moving away from the main lines and moving out into the land of pre-war terraces and it was starting to bother me.

Someone was tailing us, so just to make sure, I took the Jag on a tour of back roads for a few minutes. Then I was sure.

I nudged Laura in the ribs and she woke up. "What?"

"Know anyone with expensive tastes in German sedans?"

She squinted and blew the hair out of her face. "Eh?"

I jutted my chin at the rear view mirror. "We're being followed by a black Merc. Is it Sorin's?"

She yawned and peered forward into her side door mirror. Then, she crashed back into her chair and clasped her face in her hands. "Oh God, yes. That's Sorin's car. I'm sure of it. I recognise the number plate."

I craned my neck and took a closer look in the mirror. "Looks like there's just one man in the car."

She peered into the side mirror and squinted. "Could be Sorin. If it is, he's smaller than I thought he would be. But no sign of Luca or Stoica.

"Luca's probably still in the hospital."

"But that still leaves Stoica. I wonder where he…look out!"

An old BMW 7 series pulled out of a side street just ahead of us, turned sharply in our direction. I spun the wheel and avoided the worst of the impact but there was no time to get us fully clear. The Beamer's right front wing smashed into the front left of our car and spun us around one-eighty degrees. I turned the crumpled nose into the skid but a second impact from behind pushed us over the kerb and through a chain-link fence running around a children's park. We came to a smoking, steaming stop when the front end of our car smashed through a waste bin and into an iron bench.

Dazed and weary, I looked in the rear view mirror and saw the other two cars pull tight arcs and drive up behind us and kill their engines. The Jag was trashed.

"They're coming over," I said. "I'm going on out there to have this out."

"That's insane!" She peered in her mirror. "That's Stoica in the BMW! Aren't you going to at least take your gun?"

"No, *that's* insane, Laura. Think it through. We just crashed into a playground in the middle of a housing estate. There are probably at least a dozen phones filming us right now and someone's trying to frame me for murder. Me strolling over to these guys with a Glock in my hand is not good optics for the evening news – or a trial, if there ever is one."

I reached under the seat and pulled out the iron jack handle.

"What are you going to do then?"

"Whatever I have to. Stay here."

SIXTEEN

I was already out of the car with the jack handle pushed down through the waistband around the back of my jeans and hidden by the big leather barn coat by the time Sorin climbed out of the Merc. Stoica pushed the BMW door half-open but stayed out of sight. It was coordinated, but not tightly. They had glanced at each other a couple of times to work out the next move. Then, without taking his eyes off me, Sorin reached around his back and pulled out an early Glock. He was holding the gun at his side, pushed up against the leg of his trousers to keep it out of sight to anyone passing by. Now Stoica climbed out and walked slowly towards me. Both men were rigid and ready for action.

When they got to around six feet in front of me they stopped. Stoica's eyes made a greedy sweep of the stolen Jag, bristling when he saw Laura in the passenger seat. She sank down lower and tried to keep her head obscured by the dash. Stoica spat on the ground in front of our car and swore in Romanian.

For a second or two, everything went quiet and still. I sensed a sort of electrical charge between us and then Sorin moved, raising the Glock and pointing it at my face. I studied his face up close. So far, he'd led a hard life. Unshaven and tired looking. Purple bags the colour of ripe figs hung under each eye. A scar ran from his left ear down into the centre of his cheek, pulling in a line of red, puckered skin. A salt-shake of white in jet black hair and big, broad shoulders. Cold, dead eyes. This man had never loved or been loved and never would.

"The girl gets out of the Jag and then you drive away. That's how this ends."

I said nothing. I was too busy trying to figure out if Stoica was armed like this other bloke. I decided against it, or he would be waving it in my face right now. Neither man knew I had the cast iron jack handle stuffed down the back of my trousers.

"You think?" I said.

Sorin curled his lip like a hungry dog and twisted the Makarov until it was horizontal just like he had seen tough guys do in the movies. He looked ridiculous but he still had a loaded gun pointed at my head and it was a Glock. That meant there was no safety and the only way to de-cock it was to pull the trigger.

"Yes, I think," he said in a thick Bucharest accent. "I think so. You do as I say now."

"Hey, how's Luca? Last time I saw him he was lying on the floor covered in concrete dust and crying like a little baby."

Stoica's face hardened. "He was in the hospital for hours. You're lucky my boss here says you can live, or I'd kill you right now."

"But I did say you can live," Sorin said. "No more trouble here today. Laura gets out of the car and you drive away. You do as I say." He waved the gun in my face with a theatrical flourish. "Now."

"Make me."

Laura sank lower into the seat, now disappearing almost completely from view. That was something, at least. Meanwhile back on the road, Sorin didn't know what to do. I guessed his experience of situations like this was that people did as he said. This time was different. He turned to Stoica and told him to get Laura out of the Jaguar.

"Stay away from my car," I said. "No one touches my car."

Sorin shook his head and laughed. The moment was entertaining him but now he lowered his voice and slowed right down for emphasis. "Get the girl out of the car, Stoica."

Stoica's eyes flicked from his boss to me and then he started padding over to the Jag. I turned slowly as he walked to keep the jack handle concealed, unsure how much the barn coat was concealing its shape. Then I waited.

He got to the car and pulled on the passenger door handle a few times. How long until he noticed the smashed driver's window?

"What's the problem now?" Sorin said.

"It's locked," Stoica called back over.

Sorin turned to me. "Unlock the car."

"I can't. The keys are inside it."

He sighed and looked at his watch. The Glock he was holding at arm's length weighed well over a pound and now the muzzle was pointing at my chest instead of my face. Sorin hadn't noticed this yet. He was too busy watching

Stoica over by the Jag. In another minute or so it would be pointing almost down to the ground. Then he would realize and lift it back up again. That gave me a window.

Stoica curled his hand into a fist and pounded on the window. He'd see the open window in a minute. "Open the car, Laura!"

"No!"

"Do as he says!" Sorin screamed. "Do it or I shoot your friend here."

Laura peered over the dash at me, unsure what to do. The gun was pointing at my waist now.

Stoica said, "Wait. The window on the other side is smashed out. I can get in that side."

"Just get out of the car, Laura," I shouted. "It's all right."

She paused a beat, trying to work out what I was up to. She didn't have to think too hard about it as she had seen me stuff the iron bar down the back of my jeans. She hit the button on the dash to unlock the doors and all the lights flashed as the central locking system blipped in response.

Stoica acted fast, yanking open the door handle and reaching inside for her. That was when I moved, reaching behind my back and grabbing the jack handle. My target was the man with the gun who was now watching Stoica trying to drag the kicking and screaming woman from a car.

I threw the bar at him as hard as I could and it spun through the air like a boomerang striking him on the side of the head with the metal socket at the end. It hit him hard and he wasn't expecting it. He grunted in pain and stumbled away to his right, falling to his knees and dropping the gun as he lifted his hands to his head to work out what had happened.

What had happened is that he had taken his eyes off me for a second too long when he was distracted by the pig's ear his man was making of extricating a young woman from a stolen car. I could understand that, and I took advantage of it. Now, I took the two paces over to him and snatched the Glock up off the ground.

Stoica broke off from Laura and lunged at me. I rotated the gun in my hand and turned it into a knuckleduster. I aimed for about twelve inches behind his face and his nose was ground zero, smashing it to a pulp as my fist made an impact. He staggered back and fell onto the Jag's bonnet. He brought his hands up to his broken, bloody nose, spat a wad of blood on the road and started cursing in Romanian.

Then he staggered away from me to his car. Inside the cab, he reached into the glove compartment.

I knew he wasn't looking for a map so I ran around to his side of the car and wrenched open the door and grabbed a fistful of leather on his shoulder and dragged him out before he had a chance to get what he was looking for. When he was down on the tarmac I kicked him in the ribs with my steel toecap boot and sent him tumbling into the gutter.

I reached inside the glove compartment and found what he had been looking for – a tatty-looking Makarov semi-automatic pistol in even worse shape than Sorin's Glock. I thumbed the magazine release catch and checked how many rounds were on board and by the time I was smacking the mag back inside the grip, the guy was crawling out of the gutter and making another move towards me.

Then, a gun exploded in the quiet afternoon, almost impossibly loud. Sorin had pulled a Tokarev from an appendix holster and fired it at me. He was fast, I'll give him that. Everyone froze on the spot and smoke curled up from the barrel. A hot, burning pain stung the top of my arm and I looked down to see a rip in the barn coat's leather sleeve. I knew I hadn't taken a bullet and decided against killing him. Instead, I fired a single shot and blew the gun out of his hand. Then I fired on the Merc and took out the front two tyres.

Stoica ducked down inside the BMW as his boss scrambled behind the Merc.

Seeing our Jag was trashed, I padded around to Stoica and pushed the gun in his face. "Out, now."

He crawled away across the seats and climbed out of the passenger door on the other side of the car. Then I told Laura to get inside. She climbed into it as I ordered Stoica away from the BMW and over to his boss by the Merc. Now I swung the gun and raised it arm's length and pointed it in Sorin's face.

"I'll kill you for this," he said coolly. "You and all your family."

I said nothing and slipped down into the seat beside Laura and fired up the engine. As we raced away, I watched Sorin make a phone call on his mobile as Stoica kicked the flat tyres.

"He will, you know," Laura said.

"What?"

"Kill you and your family. He's a psycho."

"If he does, he'll die trying."

"And we need to get you to a hospital." She gently pulled open the rip in my coat sleeve and winced. My entire upper arm was slick and sticky with blood. "This is terrible."

"It's just a graze. And no hospitals."

"A motel then, and stop being such an idiot."

I fought away a smile, pulled out onto the A road and put my foot down.

SEVENTEEN

When Laura poured the alcohol on the gunshot wound I gritted my teeth and fought hard to stop moving my arm.

"Stop being such a big baby."

"Oh yeah?" I said. "When was the last time you got shot?"

She swallowed a smile and raised her eyebrows in exaggerated concentration, dabbing the wound one more time with the alcohol-soaked cotton wool. We were both sitting on the end of the bed inside a Travelodge just outside of London. She was closest to the door and the window was behind her allowing the weak daylight to illuminate her hair like a halo.

While she worked away, cleaning the wound and dressing it with the gauze, the moment slowed down almost to a stop. The room was warm, heated by a single panel convector radiator running under the window. The radiant heat rising from its cast-iron housing moved the thin curtains back and forth in the way a light summer breeze might do and the muted TV set in the corner bathed us in the crimson glow of the news studio.

The last few hours were starting to catch up with me now. Laura too, maybe, but she was much younger. As an officer in the SAS, I still had to pass demanding physical fitness tests regularly but the time required to finish them started to get more generous the older you were. Either way, I knew when I wanted a rest and one of those times was fast approaching.

"Thanks for this," I said.

She was still finishing off the dressing and spoke without taking her eyes from her work. "It's nothing. There, all done."

"Not quite. Give me your bag."

She handed it to me and I tipped its contents out on the bed.

"Hey! A woman's bag is her private business."

"Is that why she always keeps it on her and takes it everywhere she goes?"

"Maybe."

"Which is why it's the perfect location for what I'm looking for."

I was feeling through the lining. Then, I ripped the bottom of the bag open and found what I was looking for. She stared at the tiny flat white square in between my finger and thumb with horror. "Is that what I think it is?"

"Depends on whether or not you think it's an OriginGPS Micro Hornet."

"I'd got as far as GPS."

"Then yes. I thought it was odd how fast Luca found us when we were driving south of the river and my first thought was he was tracking you via your Gmail account's GPS app. Problem with that is there's a delay before it updates new data to the account. That was when I started thinking he had a serious, bespoke GPS micro tracker on you. When they pulled up behind us just now in the Merc the case was closed." I put it on the table and smashed it to pieces with the stock of my Glock. "Now he's in the dark again."

She went quiet. "Thanks for all this, Blake. Luca would have killed me if he'd caught up with me that night and you hadn't been around."

"Forget about it. We'll stop Sorin from bothering you and your dad, I promise."

She stared at me for a few seconds, inches away from my face, and then pushed her hair back behind her ears and blew out a deep sigh, eyes fixed on mine, pupil's widening. "All righty, then." She turned and walked away from me. "You should still go to a hospital and see a doctor."

"It's just a flesh wound. A graze."

She went quiet for a minute. "I can't believe they killed your friend."

"It was cyclosarin," I said. "I've been thinking about it all morning and I'm convinced."

"What's that?"

"An extremely fast-acting and highly toxic nerve agent. Russians are known to have large stockpiles of it. The agent penetrates clothes and in his case entered through the skin of his upper legs. Whoever did this must have eavesdropped on our phone call, made a note of where we were meeting and left the liquid on the bench."

"They do things like that?" Laura asked.

"Yes. Remember when they dropped the Novichok in Salisbury? It happens."

She said nothing, eyes dropping to the floor as she swept some more of her hair away from her face and hooked it back up over her ears. She reached for a plastic shopping bag on the bed behind us and pulled out a small box of sandwich bags. We'd bought them in a Tesco Metro near the motel. "What are these for?"

I took the box from her and punched open the little perforated edge. Pulling one of the bags out I held it over the dressing. "I need a shower and I don't want to get this wet. Could you tape it down over the gauze with the electrical tape we bought?"

She smiled and picked up the tape. "I should start charging for this."

"And what are your rates?"

She rolled out a few inches of tape and then bit the end off. "Standard rates."

I closed my eyes and felt her fingers taping the plastic baggy around the dressing. It was not a permanent solution but it would work for a day or two. Until this was over.

"There. Now we're done."

"Feels great. I'm going to hit the shower and then I need a nap." I got up from the bed and walked over to the bathroom. "You should consider getting a shower, too."

She paused and her face changed.

"After me, I mean."

She furrowed her brow and smiled at the same time. It looked odd. "Sure. I'll get one when you're sleeping."

*

The shower was hot and good. I stood directly under the main jet and let the water crash into my face and run down my neck. Cracking my neck to release some tension, I grabbed the soap and got to work washing myself down. I knew Laura's Romanian friends needed a little time to regroup and get angry and talk about revenge, and I had to use that time wisely. Cleaning up and getting some sleep was essential. I'd only had a couple of hours' sleep at Matt's place and that was on a sofa.

I turned the shower off and grabbed a towel. Then, using the cheap set of disposable razors we'd bought I shaved and brushed my teeth and got dressed, leaving my shoes off. Returning to the main bedroom, I saw Laura on the bed, sleeping. I considered lying down beside her but scratched the idea. It was forward and presumptuous; we had met only a few hours ago and barely knew each other.

I walked over to the bed, picked up one of the spare pillows and then returned to the chair in the corner next to the TV set. I crushed the pillow down into the back of the chair, the same way I do on commercial aircraft and then made myself as comfortable as I could. I only needed an hour to recharge and I had slept in much worse places. Much worse. I closed my eyes and tried to rub out what had happened to me in the previous hours and then I was gone.

When I woke after lunch, thin, watery light was spilling onto the carpet in front of the radiator under the cheap curtains. Laura was still fast asleep on the bed. She had pulled the covers up over her and looked peaceful. Only a few short hours since the team and I went through the skylights back in Connaught Square and I still had no idea what was going on. I wanted to change that. I rummaged around in my pocket and found the slip of paper John Grant had given me back in the park.

It was time to talk to Brookline and get some answers but fate had one more surprise. When I pulled out my phone I saw I already had a message waiting.

EIGHTEEN

I looked at the image on my phone. John Grant's dead face was staring back at me, cold and white and horribly contorted. The bloody foam around his mouth had dried into a greasy maroon patina and his bulging, bloodshot eyes were now fully glazed over. Below the picture were the words: STOP OR YOU'RE NEXT. LAST WARNING.

"What is it?" Laura asked. She had woken and was pulling herself up onto her elbows. Dust motes drifted in the air between us.

I flicked the photo away and turned the phone over. The last thing she needed to see was this. "Nothing. Just something from an old friend."

She crawled up and pushed her shoulders against the headboard. Blew some hair out of her eyes and yawned. "You seemed pretty unhappy about whatever it was."

"I said it's nothing."

"I know you're not being honest with me. It had something to do with this morning, didn't it?"

I hesitated then began typing in the numbers Grant had given me. "I have a call to make."

She shrugged. "Fine. What time are we going to Dad's?"

I switched it to speakerphone and set it on top of the TV. She looked a little annoyed I hadn't explained more about the call and what I had just seen. "Right after this call." When Brookline answered I said, "So, you're still alive then, Peter."

"I might say the same about you, Bill. Where the hell are you?"

"Taking bacon and eggs in Claridge's with a friend. How about you?"

He gave a sad laugh. "You're right not to tell me."

"Grant told me you're on the outside. Why?"

"Straight to the point, just like old Bill."

"Well?"

"I was a naughty boy and they smoked me out."

"Who's doing the smoking, Peter?"

"That's the sixty-four million dollar question."

"I don't have any time and I need answers. Gilmore and Rollins went rogue in the Russian woman's house, killed her, killed her security, killed Andy Foster and tried to kill me. I ended up in custody where two goons told me if I didn't confess they'd kill me and target my family. We parted company and from that point on, I've been running. What is this about?"

"We're being set up, old friend. You and I. D19."

Laura's eyes widened and she swung her legs off the bed. Barefoot, she stepped gingerly across the cheap carpet and went inside the bathroom and locked the door. She had left me alone with Brookline.

"Set up for what and by whom?"

"Something pretty ugly, Bill. You're better off getting out of the country. That's my plan."

"I need more than that. Tell me about Operation Wildhorse."

A long pause. "Grant told you."

"Yes, before they killed him."

"John Grant is dead?"

"As a doornail."

"Christ."

"Wildhorse, Peter. Tell me what you know."

"What I know about Wildhorse cannot be discussed like this. Trust me. We need to meet."

"Yeah, that's what Grant told me and look at what happened to him. I can send you a picture of it if you like. Someone just sent it to me. Trying to put the frighteners on me. Want me to forward it?"

"That won't be necessary, thanks. You said you were having breakfast with a friend. Do you have company?"

"Yes. A woman I met."

"It really is the same old Bill. Can we trust her?"

"What do you mean?"

"When did you meet her?"

"Last night."

"After all this went down?"

"Yes."

Another long pause. "You see my point."

"She's nothing to do with whoever is behind this, Peter. She has her own problems, believe me."

"Let's hope you're right. If we make a mistake, we're done. She could be a plant, Bill. One of them. It's a bit of a coincidence that you ran into her just after all this took off, don't you think?"

"It was still a coincidence. It was a car crash. She couldn't have faked it – she'd been drinking."

"You're the best in the division, Bill and a good friend. If you say you can trust her then I'll take your word for it but I'm not happy about it. They want to put this on us, Bill. The whole damned thing, and trust me when I say it's all too heavy to carry."

"I prefer facts to trust."

"And you'll get them. Are you still in London?"

"No."

"Where are you? General area will do."

"North of London."

Brookline went quiet. "There's a D19 safehouse in Chelmsford."

"No."

"Then where?"

"I'll call you when I have somewhere."

"The element of surprise, I see."

"It's not like that, Peter. You're the divisional commander. You know I trust you, but if we're both being hunted this has to be done a certain way. Stay on this number."

I hung up and tapped on the bathroom door. "All good?"

Laura opened the door and smiled. The phone was in her hand. "I was sitting on the side of the bath. Just staying out of your way. Sounded serious."

"It's fine. Let's get you back to your dad's place."

NINETEEN

The drive to Harlow was quiet. We stopped in Cheshunt for some burgers and ate them on the main road driving north. Stoica's Beamer was a smooth and easy ride, even with the damage to the front wing, but Sorin was going to be a problem. Truth was, a man like him wasn't ever going to leave Laura or her father alone and my involvement had only made things worse. It was up to me to end the Sorin problem.

"There it is," she said. "Next right."

Her father's home was a big, new house. Gates and portico. I guessed her father had won the haulage game and was looking forward to a soft retirement when Sorin had stepped in and changed everything. The electric gates swung open and I pulled the battered BMW up onto the smooth tarmac and killed the engine. Their house was built on a large parcel of rural land beyond a low stone wall. Beyond it, fields ran off to the horizon. A cold wind whipped over those fields and whistled around the car.

"Let me handle him," she said.

"Anything you say."

"He was never the same after mum died. This business with Luca was just the icing on the cake."

A curtain twitched in a downstairs window, then her father opened the door with a cautious smile. He was in his early sixties, a little overweight but nothing life-threatening. Receding hair greying at the temples and two days' stubble on his face. He looked tired and drawn.

"Laura, I wasn't expecting to see you."

"Hey, Dad."

Now his eyes turned to me and his face changed expression. It wasn't hard to explain. I was nearly twice her age and leaning on a seventy grand car that had clearly just been in a serious accident. If I were this guy, I'd be a hell of a lot angrier than he was.

"Who's this?"

"Blake," she said.

His smile faded completely now. He stepped out of the portico and walked over to me. A life running a trucking company wasn't an easy life. He was well-built and not afraid to square up to me and look after his girl.

"And who's Blake?"

This time, the question was aimed at me.

"Bill Blake," I said.

"He saved my life, Dad," she said. "Stop giving him a hard time."

He turned around and faced her. "Saved your *life*? What happened?"

She said nothing.

I saw his shoulders slope. "Sorin..."

"Can we please go inside?" she said. "I need a cup of tea."

He eyed me suspiciously but then rolled over. "You saved her life? Come in and get some tea, Bill Blake. My name's Dave. Dave Thompson."

*

We drank it in the front room. On the wall behind him was a picture of the family in happier days. Mum, Dad and Laura. All younger and smiling. Pre-Sorin by several good, fat years, I guessed.

"From what Laura says, Bill Blake, you really did save her life. I owe you everything. She's all I have since Susan died."

"You owe me nothing. I just did the right thing at the right time. There's no debt here."

He was quiet. Sipped his tea and choked back some tears. "That bastard did this to us. He broke me if I'm being honest."

Laura reached out and touched his arm. A daughter just letting her father know she was nearby.

"It's all right, Dad."

I said, 'Laura told me he has a place in the West End. I'm presuming he has somewhere out of the city, too. Somewhere closer to the ports."

Dave nodded. "Yes, he's based up here most of the time. Easy access to Felixstowe to keep an eye on his drugs. London is just for kicks and giggles."

"And where is this local base?"

"A farmhouse between here and Chelmsford," Dave said. "Big place. Cost a fortune, no doubt. Bought and paid for with filthy drugs money." His head dropped and he stared down at his slippers. "I am so ashamed."

"How do you get to this farmhouse?"

"No way," Laura said. "You've done enough, Bill. Just drive away and forget about all of this before he kills you."

"I can't leave things like this. I've stirred up a hornets' nest."

"Nothing will change," Dave said. "When you leave, Sorin will come around here and slap me around a bit. Luca will take Laura away again. Maybe to the farmhouse, maybe to the place in London. But we'll be alive. He won't kill us as long as I drive the drugs into the country. Simple."

"That's no way to go on living."

"It's the only way," Dave said. "And it won't be forever. I've got a plan. I'm going to sell this place up and move the two of us away. I have friends, good friends. They're in Spain. We'll move out there and change our names. We'll be fine. Sorin will forget all about us and find someone else to smuggle his drugs."

"What sort of drugs?" I asked.

"A lot of synthetic stuff," Dave said. "Also heroin. Horse, they call it. As I said, I reckon if we can just get away we'll be all right."

"Maybe, but if it's all the same with you I think I might just pay this farmhouse a visit. See if we can't sort this out once and for all."

"I don't think that's a very good idea," Laura said.

"We'll let the future be the judge of that. In the meantime, I'm going to need you both to check into a hotel you've never used before."

TWENTY

I drove Sorin's Beamer up the farm track and pulled it up outside an old garage block. The late winter's day was cold and dark. Some of the downstairs windows were lit but most were dark. Rain pattered on the roof of the car as I scanned the property. Someone was home. I guessed Sorin had regrouped his gang after what happened earlier. By now he knew he had a problem and that problem was me.

The main house was long and covered in plaster the colour of a soft melon. At both ends of a brown tiled roof was a chimney. One was dead but smoke twirled up into the sky from the other. At least I knew which end of the house they were sitting in.

I pulled my Glock from the glove box and climbed out of the car. Gun gripped in both hands and muzzle pointed at the ground, I made my way across the gravelled drive and approached the house. From the two cars in the garage block and the dead fireplace, it was safe to assume there were no more than half a dozen men in the house. Probably less. I also knew Luca had taken a year's worth of beating in the last few hours and wouldn't be up to another serious fight.

I found a dark room at the back of the house with a double-hung sash window and put the glass in with my elbow. Matt's leather barn coat took the brunt without so much as a scratch. I leaned in and lifted the catch and gently pushed up the lower sash. Brushed the smashed glass off the sill and set the gun down while I took hold of the casing with each hand and pulled myself inside the house. I was in a kitchen with old fittings and cheap laminated flooring. A hole where maybe a dishwasher should go was just a black void with pipes hanging out of it. A week's worth of plates and cutlery was stacked up all over the top of a filthy Aga solid fuel stove.

I slid the gun off the sill and moved to the door into a long narrow corridor. By now I heard the laughing. It was a low, braying noise that reminded me of pigs fighting at the trough. There was also talk, fast talk in Romanian. The house reeked of cigarette smoke and I followed the smell down to the end of the house where I found what I was looking for.

I stepped forward into a long dining room and one of the men at the table stared at me, his eyes wide like saucers. A heartbeat or two later, he told the others and they turned to see me standing in the door, the Glock trained on Sorin, still lean and unshaven and hard-looking. Behind him, I saw my reflection in some internal French doors, one slightly ajar and nothing but a dark room beyond. Stoica was one side of him and Luca the other, with his leg and hand all muffled up inside big, thick white plaster casts.

I took another step into the room. "Anyone reaches for a weapon and they're stopping a bullet."

"That's not polite, Sorin said.

"It's the way it is."

"We were just talking about you. My employer is very unhappy with what happened to his cars today. He's told me you must die."

"Sounds like a tough guy."

"Mr Zadik is the last word in tough."

"And here I was, thinking you were the big boss when you're just another monkey."

Sorin was sitting at a table in front of a half-eaten leg of beef. He took a chunk to chew and started playing with a packet of Ukrainian cigarettes and a box of matches, balancing one on top of the other and then switching them around. I had walked in here into the heart of their criminal empire and was pointing a gun in his face and he was going to show me he didn't care about that one bit. He was going to balance his cigarette packet on a box of matches.

"Where is this Zadik?" I asked.

Sorin pulled out a cigarette now and incorporated it into his game, seeing if he could stand the cigarette up on its tip like a pillar and then rest the matches on top of it. This achieved, he now placed the cigarette packet on the matches.

"You have no business with Mr Zadik."

"I asked you where he is."

"You realize, you should be grateful I have decided to talk to you. This is only because I respect the way you have handled yourself around my men. I am still going to kill you, but I will make it fast. You should be grateful for this, too. The last person I killed spent three days thinking about why it took three days for him to die."

"If you want me to die, Sorin, you have to make it happen. Right now you're just a flapping mouth."

He didn't rise to the bait. He pulled the carving knife out of the joint of beef and wiped the meat off with a cloth beside his plate. "Nobody will ever find you out here. When you're dead we'll take your body out and put it ten feet under one of the potato fields. We have a digger on the farm. Why are you here, stranger?"

"I was going to have a chat with you, but now I want to speak to Zadik."

"Maybe I can still help you."

"I doubt it. I'll talk to the engine driver, not his oily rag."

His eyes flashed with anger and he pushed his chair back and stood up, carving knife gripped in his hand. "You have no respect, stranger."

"But I have a Glock."

"I have three men."

"Too bad there are eight rounds left in this gun. You can have two each."

"That's very generous," he said. "But I am more generous. If you don't drop the gun, my associate Lazarescu will let you have all thirty rounds from the detachable drum fitted to his twelve-gauge Saiga shotgun. He's standing on the other side of those doors at the end of the room."

Maybe he was. I stalled. The Saiga was basically a shotgun version of a Kalashnikov AK47 and you rarely won an argument against it. "You think I'm stupid?"

"No, but you obviously think I am. You think I would sit around in here without any protection? Mr Zadik runs one of the biggest smuggling operations in eastern England. He has lots of enemies. He looks after his people." He raised his voice. "Lazarescu, make your presence known."

TWENTY-ONE

The French doors exploded into a thousand pieces and the clunky *chang chang chang* roar of the Saiga's gas-operated rotating bolt filled the room. Sorin scrambled to the door I had entered from while Stoica and Luca dived to the carpet beside the shattered doors. I had a fraction of a second to react. I slammed into the floor and tipped up the table. The beef and plates and knives and mustard and cigarettes flew all over the place as I took aim at the man with the Saiga and tracked him across the small room beyond the French doors. I fired on him and planted two in his back. He went down into the darkness of the other room and took the Saiga out with him.

Six rounds left. Luca had fallen to his hands and knees and was crawling out of the room into the corridor I had used to enter, dragging his plastered leg behind him. Stoica was helping him and Sorin was now standing inside the room behind the French doors. He must have accessed it from another door and he looked like he wanted blood. He ran across the room to the dead man and snatched up the Saiga. Unlike Lazarescu, he kept his head tucked down behind a chair and opened fire on me. The big, powerful gun's muzzle flashed in the darkness as rounds roared from the barrel and chewed into the upturned table and blasted out the other side, inches from me.

I had to make tracks. A Glock with six rounds wasn't up to a fight with the Saiga and I guessed Stoica and Luca were on their way to find more weapons. I snatched up the cigarettes and scrambled away from the table, keeping low and out of sight as I headed for the door. Sorin got cocky and raised his head above the chair to fire on me as I fled. The Saiga jerked and rattled in his hands as he swept the muzzle calmly and chased me out of the room. I turned and discharged another round at him, missing but driving him back into cover and then I was through into the hall and found Stoica and his brother trying to reach the stairs.

I grabbed Luca by the back of his coat, turned him and belted him across the temple with the Glock's grip and knocked him clean out. Stoica had already climbed two or three steps and now he cried out in rage and flung his leg out at me, trying to kick me in the face. I took hold of his boot, twisted it and brought him crashing down on his arse. Then I pulled him down the steps and planted the Glock's grip in the middle of his face, knocking him out cold, too just like his brother.

Sorin was screaming in Romanian and I heard him squeeze off a couple more shells from the Saiga and blow a chunk out of the staircase to my left. He was in the dining room but heading my way so I turned tail and ran outside into the cold dark.

Emboldened by my flight, Sorin was giving chase and now broke cover from the dining room and headed into the hall, screaming for my blood as he headed towards the door.

I ran to an old pickup truck parked up between the garage block and the house and ducked behind the tailgate and aimed at the rear door. On the truck's flatbed, I saw half a dozen cans of petrol poking out from under a sloppily positioned tarp. Then, Sorin's silhouette appeared in the door and he opened fire again, blasting indiscriminately into the darkness. I kept my head down and let him empty the drum. When I heard dry clicks I knew that had happened. Then I lifted the gun into the aim and aimed at his head.

"It's over, Sorin. You're out of rounds and my crosshairs are lined up on your forehead. Move and you take a bullet."

He froze on the spot, squinting as he tried to work out my location. "You can't get away with this, whoever you are."

"Don't count on the others. Lazarescu is dead and Stoica and Luca are both out cold. It's just you me and the Glock. Now drop the Saiga."

He obeyed and it clattered down on the concrete doorstep.

"Hands in the air and stay where you are."

I took one of the petrol cans and casually walked over to him. "Get back in the dining room. Nice and slow."

He turned and walked inside. When he was a few steps inside, I picked up the Saiga, folded the stock up and pushed the weapon down inside the big, generous pocket inside the barn coat. It fit like a glove. Then, I followed him in. "You should have told me where I can find Zadik. Then I'd be out of here and you and your friends would be eating your beef and smoking your cigarettes. I hate unnecessary violence. It upsets me."

"Not as much as Mr Zadik is going to upset you for doing this to his house."

"You ain't seen nothing yet, Sorin." I unscrewed the cap on the dented petrol can and the stench of the gas fumes bloomed up into the air. "Zadik's location or I torch this farmhouse with you and your friends in it."

He looked less cocky now. He took a step back and stared at the can. "You can't be serious? Who are you? What are you doing here?"

I doused everything in sight in the petrol and pulled out my lighter. Sorin's eyes widened like saucers and he took another half-step back, almost tripping over the upturned table. "You are insane!"

"You have to take a man as you find him."

I flicked the brass lid up and put the tip of my thumb on the spark wheel. "Where is Zadik?"

He looked through the door at the limp body of his unconscious associates and gave way. "All right, fine. Zadik owns a club in Chelmsford. It's called The Blue Hour. You'll find him there."

"That wasn't so hard now, was it?"

"If you go there, he will kill you."

I tossed the lighter into the heap of trash behind the table and the fumes ignited before it hit the wood. I was already gone, out the door, holding the can of petrol and slopping what was left of it up the outside walls before throwing the empty can through the window. I came away and watched Sorin through the door. He reached down and grabbed Luca around the ankles and was pulling him out of the burning hallway. He dumped him on the gravel and then went back inside for Stoica.

I backed up over to the garage block and watched the flames take hold of the old building, licking up the walls and crawling out through the smashed windows and open door. Smoke billowed from the same windows and doors, great thick plumes bubbling up into the flat dull sky. The days were short at this time of year and the sun was already down, sucking what little colour there was into a washed-out twilight.

In front of the burning house, I saw Sorin walking in a circle with a phone clamped to his ear. On the ground beside him, Stoica had come to and was trying to bring his brother round. I turned and opened the Beamer's driver door. Steering in a wide arc on the gravelled drive, I headed back down the track. When I got to the main road I turned east to Chelmsford and The Blue Hour.

TWENTY-TWO

It was full dark by the time I got to Chelmsford. Young people and some not so young people were lining up in the rain to get into their favourite clubs. I found Zadik's club and pulled up opposite in a multistorey car park on the top level. I climbed out of the car and pulled up the collar on my leather barn coat. At least by now, I thought of it as mine.

The club's façade was narrow and three storeys high. It was painted black with a flashing neon blue sign above the only door, either side of which were two heavy-set fellas with ear pieces. They wore black waterproof jackets and black beanies and had another six or so hours standing outside in the rain tonight. I waited there for an hour, smoking one of Sorin's Prima cigarettes and watching people all tarted up to the nines trailing into Zadik's meat market. A police car went past twice in that time. Maybe that was its regular route.

I walked down the car park's concrete steps and crossed the street. The club was on a slight bend and I had to wait on a traffic island while a supermarket truck drove past, trailing a dozen cars behind it. Then I joined the queue and waited to get inside. At the door, one of the bouncers raised a meaty hand and pushed it on my chest.

"You here on your own, bud?"

"What do you think?"

"No need to be sarky, mate. Just asking a question."

"Then yes. It's just me and the coat. We're looking to buy a drink and get to know each other a little better. Take our relationship to the next level."

"All right, this is a nightclub, not a comedy club. Any problems and you're outside in a jiffy."

I brushed past him and entered the building. There was a small foyer and then a staircase leading down into the club. At the bottom of the steps were toilets on my right and large black swing doors ahead of me. I pushed them open and stepped inside. Apart from Camelot in London, at least ten years had passed since the last time I had been in a club but nothing had changed. Three deep at the bar, the smell of perfume and aftershave and alcohol everywhere. Bright lights on a ceiling rig flashed and strobed on drunk people dancing on an elevated dance floor. The music was terrible and loud.

I walked to the bar. Taller and older than most of the other people here and wearing a leather barn coat with a bloody bullet tear on the sleeve, I had no trouble getting through the crowd and coming face to face with one of the barmaids. She was around twenty, with bottle-blonde hair and a tight t-shirt partially obscuring some kind of flower tattoo on her neck. She leaned forward over the bar and raised her voice.

"What can I get you?"

"I want to speak with the owner."

She looked confused for a second, expecting a simple drinks order. "I don't know about the owner, but you can talk to my manager."

"Fine." I slipped her a folded five-pound note. "This is for you."

She shrugged and smiled and made the note disappear. "That's him over there. Kevin's his name."

She indicated beyond the throng of people at the bar to a man sitting in a small booth with a handful of young men and women. He was making some thin hair go a long way with plenty of product and had a small gold hoop in his left ear. He wore a black shirt, unbuttoned to reveal part of his shaved chest and was sitting back on a semi-circular vinyl bench seat. His arms were splayed out either side of him behind the rests so each hand was holding the shoulders of the women on either side of him. On the table were several empty glasses and a bottle of champagne upside down in an ice bucket and a small piece of waxed paper beside some white powder.

I stepped over to him.

"Kevin."

He turned his head and took me in, looking me up and down. His smile faded. "Do I know you?"

"I don't think that's very likely, do you?"

Smile all gone now and arms pulled off the girls and brought forwards onto the table. "What do you want? I'm trying to enjoy myself."

I glanced at the empty wine bottle in the bucket and the cocaine. "I can see that. Special occasion?"

"Look friend, everyone here is having a good time. That's what The Blue Hour is all about. Either go and have a good time or get lost."

"Charming."

He started to get up. I leaned forward and put my hand on his chest and pushed him back down into his seat. Hard.

"Get your hands off me!"

"I need to speak to Zadik and I'm in a hurry. Where is he?"

He laughed. Tried to look cool and regain some dignity. "You're having a giggle, mate. No one just comes in here and demands to speak to Bogdan Zadik. He's a busy man."

"Yeah, and I know why. Smuggling Afghani raw hide into the country must take up a lot of his time."

He shifted uncomfortably in his seat and looked around to see who was listening to us. The coast was clear but he told the women to disappear. When they were out of sight, he said, "If you're a copper…"

"Do I look like a police officer, Kevin?"

He lowered his voice. "What do you want here?"

"To speak with Zadik. Did you hear what I said about being in a hurry?"

He sighed. "There's a Platinum Lounge here, for the more upmarket clientele. Zadik is up there now, but there's security on the door and you ain't getting anywhere near dressed like that. You've got no tie, no suit jacket and a hole in your coat."

"And how does one find the Platinum Lounge?"

"Did you hear what I…"

I reached down and grabbed a fistful of his shirt and pulled him roughly towards me, halfway up out of his seat. "Where is the Platinum Lounge, Kevin?"

He pointed over to the elevated dancefloor, still packed with people. "There, over there. The purple door."

"Thanks." I pushed him down in his seat. "You're the only one who knows I'm going up there. If you call the cops or any security on me, I will come to your house one night and make you regret it. Got it?" I carefully lifted the flap of the big long leather barn coat and showed him the Saiga sitting in the inside pocket. Only the tip of the big, ugly perforated muzzle brake was visible, but it seemed to leave an impression on him. His eyes widened and he gave a shallow nod. Then I knocked him out with a powerful haymaker. As I stepped away from him, one of the women looked at his unconscious body slumped down on the bench seat and then up at me. I shrugged "Too much coke. A man's got to keep his motor clean."

I walked away from her towards the purple door. I was able to avoid the dancefloor by tracking around the edge of it and then walking three steps at the side of it. Then, I pushed open the purple door and the vibe changed. The music was better and so was the lighting – a nice mellow blue from a neon strip running around the ceiling. Even the two goons standing either side of the private door inside were dressed in smart black suits with white shirts and ties. The soft purple lighting shone on their shaved heads.

One of them clocked me and raised his hand. "No way, Tiger."

The other one also checked out my clothes and shook his head. "Suit and tie, fella. Go home and get dressed properly. Then we might consider letting you in."

"I need to speak with Mr Zadik. It's personal."

The first one tapped a small piece of laminated A4 paper stuck to the wall. "This is the Platinum Lounge. We have a dress code."

The other guy slowed his speech like he was talking to an idiot. "In. Here. Dress. Code. Go. Away."

"But it's just a flying visit. I don't want to spend any time in the lounge."

The one on my right lowered his voice. "Are you one of Eddie Fraser's boys come for the deal?"

"No."

"Then go home, stranger, before things get spicy."

"Who says I have a home? I just want five minutes with Zadik."

They both shrugged. "Then you have a problem."

"How's that then?"

"Because we're not letting you in," the first one said. "And if you don't get lost we'll throw you out the back and deposit you in one of the garbage cans."

"What, a couple of cupcakes like you two?"

They stepped forward. "Now you really do have a problem, fella."

"No," I said flatly, curling my hands into tight fists. "You're the ones with a problem."

TWENTY-THREE

They both came at me at the same time, cocky and sure of the outcome. I read it in their weary, cynical eyes. Handling clowns like me was their meat and potatoes. Another day another dollar. They made the obvious moves, learnt long ago in their security training, trying to spin me around and pin my arms behind my back. Too bad I knew what was coming.

Leaving the Saiga inside the barn coat, I fired a jab into the first guy's jaw and cracked his head back against his shoulder. He wasn't expecting it but handled it well. Tottering for a second and then coming at me with growing anger in his eyes. The other one was still reaching for my arms. I drove an elbow onto his face and broke his cheekbone as I spun around and brought my other hand up into the first guy's nose. It splattered across his face like a tomato and now the second one with the big swollen cheek was bringing his hand up. Not to hit me but to speak into his palm mic.

I grabbed his hand, yanked him forward and crashed my forehead into his nose, breaking that one too. Then I snatched hold of the wire leading to the palm mic and pulled it hard, ripping it through his sleeve and throwing it to the carpet. The other guy was coming up behind me when the

137

mic guy rotated on his hips and threw a meaty fist at me. I dodged away and let it fly past me into the face of his associate, knocking him out.

One down, one to go. He was a big guy with heavy fists but he was slow and his confidence had been shaken. His normal method of dealing with trouble had been undermined and now tempered further by his mate going down like a sack of broken bricks. With no mic and a local reputation to ride on, he had no choice but to come at me again. He took a second to get his breath back and threw a couple of jabs out. I bobbed and weaved my way out of it like Bill Demspey against Jess Willard back in 1919. The easy deflection seemed to wind him up because now he straightened up and stepped back and strutted around like a rooster for a few seconds.

"I'm putting you down tonight!"

He came at me and I punched him in the ribs, hard. He doubled over, gasping for air. I was about to finish him off when another doorman stepped into the small foyer. He was carrying a baseball bat, some kind of old faithful they kept in reserve for the truly naughty boys. He charged towards me and swung the bat without warning.

It was meant to kill me, and if it had hit me on the head it would have done just that. Maybe in the movies people get up from being hit with a bat, but not in real life. A bat like this weighs at least thirty-one ounces and swung by a guy with this guy's arms it would deliver maybe eight thousand pounds of force. I know from experience it takes just over five hundred pounds of force to break a human skull, so if that piece of finely crafted ash hit me where he was aiming it was only going to end one way.

I ducked again and heard the bat whistle past me, maybe an inch from the side of my head. With the bat halfway through its arc, I knew his ribs were vulnerable, so I spun around and planted a hefty uppercut in the centre of his ribcage. We all heard the snapping sound as one of the ribs gave away and cracked, and now he was howling in pain by the time the bat reached its zenith. Instinct drove him to drop it on the ground and clutch at his broken rib.

I snatched up the bat and felt its weight in my hands. The other guy looked at me with confusion as I assessed who take out first. The obvious choice was the wounded man with the cracked ribs, so I swung the bat into his stomach. When he doubled over in pain I delivered a hefty kick that struck him in the face and knocked him out, cold as ice. The other guy fitted an ugly brass knuckle duster on his hand but looked scared and I guessed his mate was the ringleader. With the head cut off the snake, he had no one left to lead him into battle.

I had no such problems. With one arm, I swung the bat around in an arc and caught its smooth wooden barrel in my left hand. "Who wants his head to be a fly ball?"

Knuckles darted forward. The blue light from the neon strip running around the top of the small room glinted on the brass knucks as he powered them toward my face with all he had. I had already anticipated the attack, sidestepping the move and swinging the bat around into him. The blow struck him on the right side of his body just under the

139

swinging fist and smashed more than one of his ribs. He heaved out a grunt of pain and lashed out with his other arm.

I spun the bat around one-eighty until I was holding the barrel in my right hand and the grip in my left. I brought my right hand around so it was cupping the end cap and then drove the bat's knob up into his throat. I was being gentle with him, not wanting a genuine murder charge following me around along with everything else. I pulled the strike back at the moment of impact so it frightened him but never crushed his windpipe.

It worked. He dropped the knuckle duster and brought his hands up to his throat to check why he was in so much pain. I landed the bat in his undefended stomach and he curled up like a worm, coughing and spluttering and crashing down in the carpet not a million miles away from his mate. But he had more to give, and to my astonishment he crawled back up to his knees and then up to his feet and started padding over to me, blood all over his face and his chest heaving up and down hard.

"You my son, are dead."

TWENTY-FOUR

He moved on me again, telegraphing it on his face five seconds before moving. I was standing there waiting for it like an old bus. Then, I grabbed his throat and hooked my boot behind his ankles and swept his feet out from under him. On his way down, I helped him on his way with a final punch to the face. It landed just north of where I wanted and I caught my knuckles on his brow bone. It hurt, but he was out for the count. I dragged him over to the other guys and dumped him face down on the carpet. Then I dropped the bat, slid the bolt on the door leading out to the main club and stepped over their bodies on my way to Zadik's private party.

Through the doors and I was standing in a plush carpeted area at the bottom of another staircase. Three young women in cocktail dresses were standing around outside the ladies room drinking and sharing a laugh. They stopped talking and looked at me with suspicious eyes.

"Looking for the private party," I said.

"Up the stairs on the right," one of them said. "Silver door."

"It's platinum," said another. "Not silver. That would cost too much."

"Thanks. You should brush up on your metallurgy."

"Eh?"

I ignored her and took the stairs three at a time. I felt the Saiga swinging around inside the barn coat and pulled it in closer to my body. No sense tipping your hand too early. I reached the top of the second staircase and pushed open the sparkly, brushed chrome door the girls downstairs had described. Inside was another dancefloor, but much more upmarket. The night was still young, but most of the people in here were already drunk or high or maybe a bit of both. I scanned the busy dance floor for a moment and then caught sight of the men I was looking for. They were sitting in a booth on a dais at the back of the room, surrounded by fawning women and several empty bottles of champagne were littered on and around the table.

I walked slowly through the people on the dance floor and made my way over to the table. A man with a long-ago broken nose and two cauliflower ears was talking to another man in a sharp black suit and slicked-back sable black hair shining with grease. I presumed the ugly one was Eddie Fraser, and the guy in the black suit was Zadik. He was holding court like a renaissance king, fingers full of rings and a laugh like a jackal.

I walked over to the table and Eddie Fraser's eyes swivelled over to me as I approached. A big guy standing at his side moved to block me and I elbowed him out of the way. He stepped back in towards me but I had already caught Fraser's eye.

"I've got a delivery for Bogdan Zadik," I said.

The two bouncers on either side of the booth bristled and moved towards me. Fraser glanced at Zadik and then back over to me. He pushed the women away and sat up straight on the leather bench. "That's funny, I don't see no delivery."

Zadik laughed.

"It's right here," I said, holding out my hand.

He leaned in and peered at the hand. His mouth twisted into a sneer. "You're taking the piss. Now get lost."

I curled my hand into a fist and piled it into Fraser's face as if I was trying to punch through the plaster behind his head. The impact smashed his nose down into a bloody pulp and knocked his head back hard against the chrome rim running around the top of the red leather bench seat. His eyes rolled back in their sockets and then he passed out. Everyone around the table stared in disbelief and then the two security guys rushed towards me.

I looked at Fraser's unconscious head lolling over his shoulder with his tongue hanging out of his mouth like the town drunk. "Looks like he can dish it out, but he can't take it."

The bouncer closest to me lunged forward and swung a wild haymaker in my general direction. I caught his hand in mid-air and twisted his thumb back around against his wrist, snapping the bones and making him cry out and drop to his knees.

The second man stepped into the fight, but I warned him off. "Back off. I can break your wrist just as easily as this guy's."

The small group looked from the unconscious Eastend gangster on the bench seat down to the bouncer on his knees on the carpet and then over to Zadik. No one knew what to say, but Zadik looked at the man in the wrist-hold and then up to me. "What's your business here, stranger?"

"I'm taking care of it right now."

"Seems to me you just made the biggest mistake of your life."

"Oh yeah?"

"Yeah."

Zadik got to his feet, shouting at the man beside him. "Give me your knife! I want to cut him."

"Take it easy, Zadik."

He snatched the switchblade from the big man and slashed it in the air in front of my face. "I don't give a shit who you are, asshole. I know only this. No one comes into my club and takes out their aggression on my business associates. You're going to the hospital tonight, friend. Say goodbye to your face."

He stepped forward and raised the knife. It was showtime. I released the bouncer's wrist, kicked him away from me, lifted the front panel of the barn coat and whipped out the Saiga. It was in my hands, raised into the aim and finger on the trigger before Zadik had completed his next step. Now, he reversed course. Wild, staring eyes narrowed as he took in the big gaping hole at the end of the Russian shotgun. Maybe he recognised it from the farmhouse.

"You're making a big mistake, friend!"

I unfolded the stock of the Saiga and pushed it into my hip and ripped off a short burst into the plaster above their heads. The fully automatic weapon turned his wall to mince as I raked it with shells in a blaze of strobing muzzle flashes. Zadik dived under the table for cover and his goons scattered like sheep as I shredded the feature wall in a few seconds. The empty cases spat out of the extraction port in the side of the dust cover and rolled away behind my boots as I swept the weapon from side to side to ensure good coverage of devastation.

Everyone on the dancefloor screamed and stampeded for the exits. Zadik was still cradling his head in his hands. That's when I shot out the legs on the table and brought it crashing down on his head, knocking him clean out. Keeping a handful of ammo safely inside the weapon, I stopped firing and let the dust settle.

Hot smoke twirled from the holes on the black matte muzzle brake. I just stood there. Only Zadik's small group were still in the private lounge. Fraser and Zadik were unconscious. The bouncers were crawling up out of the wreckage, stunned and bewildered by the display of sheer destruction they had just witnessed. A chunk of plaster peeled off the ceiling and smashed on top of the broken table, breaking some of the champagne glasses.

I rested the Saiga's barrel on my shoulder and walked over to the bouncer with the broken wrist. He was up on his knees now, staring up at me with burning hate in his eyes.

"When your organ grinder wakes up, you tell him not to go anywhere near Laura Thompson or her father ever again, or next time we meet I won't bring my manners, got it?"

Before he could reply, I delivered a hefty jab into the side of his head and knocked him out clean. He slumped to the black carpeted floor in a heap. The other bouncer and the rest of them stared at him in disbelief. I turned, put my free hand in my pocket and walked slowly across the dance floor to the exit.

TWENTY-FIVE

"Hey, Peter. It's Bill."

"The wanderer returns."

I signalled left and pulled onto the main road. I was driving Stoica's BMW out of Chelmsford on my way back to Harlow. I had already called Laura and her father at the hotel and made sure they were all good and now it was time to set up a meet with Brookline.

"I have a place we can use."

"I'm listening."

"It's near Harlow."

"What the hell are you doing out there?"

"I just had to clear up some business in Essex."

"In the middle of all this?"

"I had no choice. I'd put someone's life at risk. This place is not on any radar. Not D19, not any other part of the SIS."

"I can be there in two hours."

"Good."

I gave him the location of a junction surrounded by flat farmland and drove out there and waited for him. Out here, a car's headlights could be seen for miles and when he turned up I was able to track him and make sure he hadn't been tailed.

"You made it."

"Talk about bleak."

"It's good farming country, Peter. If you left the city once in a while you might appreciate it."

"I take it we're abandoning my car now and going in yours?"

"Right."

*

Dave Thompson's house was like a fan oven by the time we got there. I guessed he had forgotten to turn off the central heating before I rushed him and his daughter out of the door earlier in the day. I cracked the window, turned the thermostat down to nothing and took off my shirt. The blood from Fraser's exploding nose had dried a dark black colour across the front and I needed a fresh one but I wasn't happy about raiding Dave's house for clothes so I stayed in what I was wearing.

I put a frozen pizza through the microwave and we sat in the dining room around the back of the house. I was hungry and ate the first slice in seconds.

"Why was I set up, Peter?"

"Because of Wildhorse."

"I'm hearing that word a lot these days. What does it mean?"

"Wildhorse is a highly classified military intelligence operation. As heavy as it gets."

"Keep talking. I can eat pizza and listen at the same time."

"Things are not as they seem, Bill. Everything you believe in is about to be blown apart. The first thing you need to know is that Wildhorse not only goes to the very top but is strictly limited to the very top. As far as I know, less than a dozen people know about it and each of them will do anything to keep it that way."

"A dozen people plus you, or are you in the dirty dozen, too?"

"No, I am not. I am not supposed to know about this. And I wish I did not know about it." He spoke slowly, cautiously. He had stopped eating his half of the pizza and was rubbing his temples. "They have killed and will kill as many times as they must to limit knowledge of this operation."

"To keep the Wildhorse tied down?"

He nodded once.

"So, how do you know about it?"

"Me and John Grant got suspicious about some terrorist chatter we'd picked up in Damascus."

"Go on."

"We started to look into it and on our travels, we ran into a journalist working for The Guardian. He never told us how he'd got hold of the thread, but he was onto something too. The same thing. Wildhorse."

I finished my pizza and gestured at his. "You mind?"

"Knock yourself out."

"Thanks. What's this journalist's name?"

"Osborne. Miles Osborne."

"I've read his column. He's big on civil liberties."

149

Brookline managed a sour laugh. "Yeah."

"I'm still in the dark here, Peter. I need to know about Wildhorse and why I seem to be the leading man in it."

"Listen to me carefully, Bill. This is all about a power struggle. Internal politics. Departmental internecine warfare, and it's getting bloody. You remember the terror attack in the London Docklands a few months ago?"

"Of course. Forty-two people died." I thought back to the devastating images of the explosion and the heart-rending stories of the victims. The attack had been the last of three similar bombings over the summer, the first in Luton and the second in Liverpool.

"When the ash was still settling, I got a phone call from Viktoria Travkin in the Russian FSB. She had something very interesting to say about it."

"In my experience, the Russian secret service usually does have something interesting to say about most things. What was it this time?"

"You know who Evgeny Leonov is?"

"He's the Russian ambassador in London."

"Yes he is, and Viktoria told me that Ambassador Leonov had informed our secret service twenty-four hours in advance of the attack."

I swallowed the pizza in my mouth and threw the half-eaten slice back onto the plate. "Keep talking."

"Viktoria wanted to know why we had nothing to stop it."

"How did she know Leonov had told our side?"

"This is where the veil starts to draw down. She was given that information by a junior member of the Russian Ministry of Foreign Affairs working in London. That woman's name was Natalia Zakharova."

My blood ran cold. "The woman we were sent arrest?"

He nodded slowly. "Leonov found out Travkin had spoken with me and contacted someone inside the British Foreign Office. It was then I decided to get Zakharova to a safehouse as she was the source of the information and I was worried about her safety. At some point, the plans were intercepted and Gilmore and Rollins were ordered to kill her and you, covering the whole thing up in the process and frame me for it."

"How?"

"They wanted to make it look like I'd been passing intel to Zakharova and wanted her out of the way. In reality, she had been passing info to us, as I have just explained."

"But why me?"

"Because of your links to me, Bill. You and I are close. We were in the Paras together and we're in the SAS together. We joined D19 only months apart. I'm your CO. They know I'm looking into this and they have to bring me down. You are how they get to me. The narrative is already written. The world believes Zakharova was a Russian diplomat and Moscow isn't going to challenge this because she was an undercover agent working illegally in the UK. Our side will tell the world I ordered you to kill her because I had been in a relationship with her and passed intel to her on the side.

So, the story is, I ordered you to kill her in the raid because she had started blackmailing me."

"I'm not liking the sound of this, Peter."

He fell silent and began searching through his suit pockets for a cigarette. "If you don't like what you have heard so far, the rest I have to tell you is really going to turn your stomach."

"How much more is there?"

"Lots, and it gets worse. Much worse, and the only way to stop this is to blow it wide open."

"Sunlight is the best disinfectant?"

"Something like that, or in this case, public exposure. Right now, only a handful of people who want to bring this thing down and are still alive are in the know. Me, you, Mark Shepherd and Miles Osborne."

"Where is Mark?"

"He got out when I did. Normal protocols so no locations. He doesn't know where I am and I don't where he is. Maybe his place in Wiltshire, maybe not. In the past, he talked about a cottage in Suffolk, too. Mark's not going to take this lying down any more than we are, but have to make it public first. Right now we're punching above our weight, so we have to get more numbers. That's where Osborne comes in. He's planning a major exposé to run in The Guardian over the next few weeks, but it's risky. He told me the editor has already been contacted by someone in the intel community and told there's a DSMA Notice stopping him printing anything about it."

A Defence and Security Media Advisory Notice was the British Government's way of 'advising' media outlets not to run a story on national security grounds. The official narrative is that they are merely requests, but everyone on the inside knew when a serious story needed crushing, it got crushed, usually by an informal telephone call alongside the DSMA Notice. Given what Brookline had already told me, it was no surprise that Wildhorse was being covered over in this way.

"Are they going to heed the advice of the DSMA Notice?"

He shook his head. "I don't think so, and right now only Osborne, his editor and you and I know that. It's going to run sometime in the next few weeks and when it does the government will fall."

"Christ almighty, Peter. How the hell did we end up in the middle of this?"

"We're special operators in the most elite secret service division of the SAS, Bill. D19. It goes with the territory. Operators get burned. Operators get disavowed. Operators get silenced. Now it's our turn."

"I don't think so. Where is Osborne?"

"I don't know, and he doesn't know where I am, for obvious reasons. I can tell you we're collating our material and evidence and stashing it in the same safety deposit box in Central London. We need to get there, get the evidence, call Osborne and go to his editor. The sooner the story goes live on their website and print editions, the sooner we can sleep at night."

"But you said this will bring the government down. Do we want to be responsible for that?"

"What you now know about Wildhorse is just the tip of the iceberg. When you find out the rest you'll want the government to burn, not just fall."

"What the hell does that mean?"

"I put some papers in there a few hours ago, just before I drove up here to meet you. Not even Osborne knows about them. It's… truly awful stuff, Bill."

He shifted in his chair and blew out a deep breath. I saw a broken man who needed a good friend, and then I froze. Time slowed. A bright, burning flicker of red light had slid onto his suit jacket and was tracking up his body. It glided over the seam of his jacket and onto his white shirt, up to his throat and cheek and stopped in the centre of his forehead. I recognised the light as a red dot laser scope and knew what came next.

"Peter!"

But it was too late to save him.

TWENTY-SIX

The whole thing had taken less than a second for the pinprick of red light to track up his body, reach his head and blow half his skull off. Blood and brain matter exploded onto the wall behind him and a red mist hung in the air. Then, a fraction of a second later I heard the sharp cracking report of the weapon, a heavy-duty sniper's rifle. The killer was close.

Brookline was dead and the red light was on the wall, then the carpet, and tracing up my leg and body. I dived behind the dining table as the sniper fired the second shot. The round blew a football-size chunk of the table into matchwood but missed. I reached up and snatched the Saiga from the table top and slammed down onto the carpet on my back. I swung the shotgun into the aim and blew out the overhead light, plunging the room into darkness.

I kicked the table onto its side with my boot and then crawled up behind it and peered through the large French doors at the end of the room. The two sniper's rounds had punched a couple of neat holes in the double-glazed glass and left two impressive spider-web fractures in the panes. Through the glass was nothing but darkness lit by a single streetlight a few hundred yards away. If I wanted to get closer to the sniper, I had to get outdoors.

I moved into the kitchen, smacked the light off and opened the back door, immediately tucking the Saiga in close to my body and throwing myself onto the rear lawn. I was right to be cautious. By the time I hit the wet ground a third shot exploded in the night and took out the top glass panel of the kitchen door. The sniper had expected me to come out looking for him. I was expecting him to fire again and had taken note of the location of the gun's report. Whoever he was, he was in the lane running along the back of the house a hundred or so yards away.

I pulled my head down and kept in nice and tight to the hedge on the side of Dave Thompson's long garden. At the end of the garden were a summerhouse and a fence made of trellis panels with an arch in the middle. I ran through the arch and slammed up against the back fence. I had a fleeting thought the killer was one of Bogdan Zadik's men. Maybe he had a more extensive network than I thought. Maybe he had people watching the house. No. This was Wildhorse. If it was Zadik I would have taken the first bullet back in the dining room.

I heard footsteps crunching on gravel. Fast, heavy footfalls receding into the night. The sniper was retreating, probably trying to reach a vehicle on standby. I scrambled through an elderberry hedge and fell out on the lane just in time to hear a bullet tracing past my head. It ripped through the foliage behind me and buried itself in a tree trunk. I whipped up the Saiga and returned fire with a rapid *chank-chank-chank* and blasted his vehicle with the shotgun shells.

He tucked down behind his vehicle for cover and returned fire. A bright flash lit the night and then a loud explosion rang out. A large chunk of the hedge beside me exploded as another round ripped through it. I moved to the other side of the lane and tucked down in the ditch and fired again. I had pulled the trigger and fired at least half a dozen shotgun shells but it was over maybe seventy yards so most had missed. Only the last two found their mark and spat lead shot all over the rear panel of his vehicle. He'd had enough. He fired off another couple of rounds while jogging back to the car. Then he threw the gun into the car and took off up the lane, screeching around a bend up ahead. I was too late. Peter Brookline's killer was long gone, but I still had Osborne.

TWENTY-SEVEN

The BMW's straight-six petrol engine hummed gently as I drove south back into London. Lit only by the soft amber lighting of the dash, the car's cabin offered a relaxing, temporary safe haven from the maelstrom preparing to engulf me. I had to call Laura and make sure she was safe. Knowing what I knew now about the nature of the Antonescu brothers and Sorin and Bogdan Zadik, she and her father could be in greater danger than I thought.

"Laura, it's Bill."

She hesitated before replying. "Are you all right?"

"I'm fine. I'm calling to find out if you and your Dad are still all good."

"We're fine. Dad's watching TV. I was reading the local news on my phone. There was a report that Sorin's farmhouse burned down. Was that you?"

"It was probably just bad wiring."

"And what about the club? They're saying there was some kind of terror attack at a Chelmsford nightclub called The Blue Hour. Belonged to some bloke called Zadik. Or was that bad wiring too?"

"Turns out Sorin isn't the man at the top of the drug-running operation they sucked you and your dad into.

That's a man named Bogdan Zadik. Luca ever mention him?"

"Not at all. What the hell have you done?"

"I handled Zadik. I don't think he'll be sending any of his men to bother you anymore, but it's important you keep a low profile for the time being in case he's stupider than I thought."

"You burned his house down and shot up his nightclub, Bill!"

"A man like that knows only violence, Laura. I warned him off you. You and your father should be able to go back to your lives now. If Zadik has any sense he'll tuck tail and run. Find someone else to run his drugs."

"But he doesn't have any sense. He's a psycho."

"I made it clear if he goes near you or your father, it'll be the last thing he ever does."

She went quiet.

I said, "But you should stay out in the sticks for a while now. Keep away from London, especially anywhere Luca spends time. Don't get sucked back in. Help your dad rebuild his business. For now, you stay at the hotel."

"But what about you?"

"I have some business of my own to attend to. I need to speak to a man about a dog."

"Can't you just say it straight for once?"

I smiled in the darkness of the cab. "You say that like you know me."

"I think I'm beginning to."

159

"Fine. The man I need to speak with can help me clear my name, but it's vital I talk to him fast. Before dawn. He's in danger."

"Are you in danger?"

"I've been in danger for years, Laura. You need to stay away from people like me."

"You saved my life. I need to stay away from people like Luca."

"We can talk later. I need to make another call. If you don't hear from me again after this call, you are to forget me and move on with your life as if I never existed."

"But…"

I cut the call and used the phone to access the internet and looked for Miles Osborne's number, but after a good search, I found nothing. I guessed either he had deleted any reference to himself he could find or someone who wanted him dead was already putting him into the memory hole. No phone numbers or addresses anywhere. Then I had an idea.

I accessed The Guardian's website and found his latest column. It was a piece on the government's latest attack on civil liberties, increased covert surveillance of civilians and the erosion of trial by jury. The state was becoming monstrous, he wrote. Needs to be reined in. Corrupt police and bent judges. Politicians on the take. Below the line were hundreds of public comments. He had replied to dozens of them, thanking supporters and bolstering his arguments against dissenters. I wondered just who those dissenters might be.

The latest reply from Osborne was just over an hour ago at just after midnight, so I decided to set up an account and leave a message under the username PaddingtonBeat0200. In the cold darkness of the car, I rapidly typed the short message into the forum and then hit 'post'.

Could they drag you away, Miles?

I can stop them dragging you away.

Look at me closely.

Any investigative journalist worth his salt ought to be able to work that one out. Especially if he was involved with a covert government operation named Wildhorse. I just prayed no one else could.

TWENTY-EIGHT

A major road accident on the A10's southbound carriage had meant a diversion around the North Circular until Greenford where I finally turned left and entered London on the Great Western Avenue, cruising through White City at just after one in the morning. The streets were quiet and a gentle drizzle softened the night and formed little haloes around the orange street lights. I cruised past lonely drifters lost in the small hours. I checked the fuel gauge and saw I was running on fumes. I turned the heater down and thought a lot about what had happened to me in the last few hours.

The raid. The arrest. Crashing into Laura on the bridge. The murders of John Grant and Peter Brookline, both good men who had served their country with courage and pride. Operation Wildhorse. I rubbed my eyes and pushed the car along Westway. I knew the area well, but the memories of this place were old and rusty. Maida Hill. Westbourne Green. Then, I pulled onto the offramp and swept around under the fly-over and over Westbourne Bridge. Then I was in Paddington. This was family turf.

I wasn't too concerned about Stoica getting a ticket, so I pulled up on some double yellow lines near the station and left the car. Collar up against the cold, I stalked across the road and checked my watch. Nearly 0200. I knew what Osborne looked like from his picture on The Guardian website, or at least what his face looked like. Thin with a mop of messy black hair and wire-rimmed spectacles. By 0210 I was sure he hadn't read the message below his column, or worse, he had been intercepted by someone on the inside who had. At 0215 my concerns were gone. Osborne had shown up and was trying to hide inside the large hood of a baggy cagoule.

I looked behind him and saw no one was following. The CCTV cameras in the area weren't swivelling in his direction when he walked. Maybe, he had got here without being tailed. I crossed the road and walked up behind him. Coming alongside, with the foyer of the Hilton London Paddington Hotel on our right, I spoke.

"You got my message then."

He jumped. He wasn't a big man and looked like he'd blow over in a light breeze.

"Keep walking."

"Who are you?"

"My name is Blake. I just spoke with Peter Brookline about Wildhorse."

He stopped and turned to me. I kept walking.

"I said keep moving, Miles."

"Sorry."

He shuffled along the pavement until he had caught up with me. "You know Peter Brookline?"

"I knew him. Someone shot him dead a few hours ago."

His face paled inside the wet hood. "Oh my God."

"And we're next if we don't get your story out."

"I can't believe this is happening. Where are we going?"

"I have a car unless it's been clamped."

"And then what?"

"And then we go to your safety deposit box and get the goodies. After that, I'm going to need twenty minutes in a room with your editor."

"With Max? He's not sure about any of this anymore. He has a family. A wife and kids. He's been getting threatening phone calls telling him to stay off it."

"I just want to talk to him."

"It's getting too risky."

"This won't go away unless we blow it open, Miles. You know that."

We got to the car and climbed inside.

"Exactly who are you, and why are you trying to help me?"

"I worked with Peter in D19. Did he talk to you about D19?"

"A little."

"D19 are a section of the British SAS Regiment that sometimes works alongside the British SIS. I have never been a member of British intelligence, MI5, MI6 or anything else you can think of. Peter and I were both pure military. Army. There's a big difference."

"Is there?" he asked cynically.

"Yes," I said flatly. "I'm a soldier, not a spy. And D19 doesn't officially exist. It doesn't really exist even within the SAS."

He went quiet and started to fiddle with his phone.

I said, "Peter told me this safety deposit box contains information both he and you had collected on the sly concerning something called Operation Wildhorse."

"Hence your use of the old expression to lure me out here tonight. That was clever."

"Maybe, but not if the enemy worked it out. It didn't exactly need the Enigma machine to decipher it. It was all I could come up with at the time. That's why we're getting out of here." I fired up the engine and pulled out of the side street. "Where is the safety deposit box?"

"How do I know I can trust you?"

"I was wondering when you'd ask me that. You can't know. I can't ask you to call Peter and check me out. You have to just trust me, Miles."

"You could kill me when we get to the box."

"I lifted my barn coat flap and showed him the Saiga. "I could put the muzzle of this gun into your midriff and order you to take me there or else. I didn't do that, did I?"

His wide eyes stared with horror at the big ugly gun. "No. What the hell is that thing?"

"It's our backup. Where am I driving, Miles?"

"Mayfair. I'll give you directions. What did Peter tell you about the contents of our dossier?"

"Everything he could before he was killed. That's not much, by the way. He told me it would shock me and he knows I'm not easily shocked. Before he died, he told me he put something else in there, something not even you know about."

"I think I know what that might be," he said nervously.

"What?"

"I'm not sure. I don't want to say anything until I see it. Call it my insurance policy in case you're not who you say you are. But I think you need to prepare yourself for something truly horrific, Blake."

TWENTY-NINE

"Why are we waiting?"

I said, "What?"

"We should get in there, grab the dossier and get out of here."

We were parked up outside the building Osborne and Brookline had used to stash their Wildhorse research. It was a 24-Hour company named Metropolis Safe Deposits not far from Grosvenor Square and I was watching the front door through a rain-streaked windscreen.

"We're watching to see who has an interest in visiting a place like this at half two in the morning. If anyone shows up, I'll bet you a pound to penny they're connected to Wildhorse."

"But we've already been here for twenty minutes."

"And we'll stay here until I'm satisfied the place isn't under any surveillance. Never be in a rush to get yourself killed."

He went quiet again. "What about you, Blake? Do you have any family to look after?"

"Not really."

"What does that mean?"

"It means I don't like to talk about myself."

"Fair enough. I just wondered if…"

"I was married once, but she's dead now."

"I'm sorry. I was married too, but we divorced."

"I know."

He looked at me. "From my column?"

"No, I had your entire house and all electronic devices bugged a week ago."

His jaw dropped. "You did what?"

"Of course from your column, Miles."

He relaxed back into the seat. "Is that army humour?"

I shrugged. "It's my humour. You need to look out for it. It flies pretty low."

"What rank are you?"

"Half-colonel, but I'm thinking by dawn I'll be on civvy street again. C'mon – I think we're good to go. Let's go and get the dossier."

*

We walked across the wet street and up some steps at the front of the building. Osborne used a plastic key-card to gain access to a small marble lobby. He opened an internal door with the same card and then we were inside a kind of vault lined with hundreds of small steel boxes.

"We're over here," he said. "Number 514."

He opened the box and withdrew a slim manila folder, creased at the corner, smudged ink writing on the front: Wildhorse.

"We have it."

Without asking, I took it from him and opened it up. "You recognise these documents?"

He peered over my shoulder. "Most of them. Some are my work, some are Peter's. Not this one, though – this must be the new one he added today. Bloody hell…"

"Bloody hell, indeed," I said. "This is a list of names of men and women connected in some way to Wildhorse and it looks pretty substantial to me."

"I count at least five government ministers and – is that *the* Michael Mulgrave?"

"The Foreign Secretary? I don't know any other people with that name in the government, do you?"

"No, I do not. This just got much more serious, Blake."

I was still flicking through the paperwork. Then I found a short, typed memo from the foreign secretary to a name I didn't recognise – a civil servant, maybe. It seemed to imply Mulgrave himself had advanced personal knowledge about the terror attack in Docklands just the same as the intel service. "This is the true horror you were talking about in the car, right?"

He nodded. "Yes, it is. The British Foreign Secretary and third highest-ranking member of the Cabinet knew twenty-four hours in advance that Docklands was going to be hit. This dossier proves it and a lot of other things as well. The question is *why* he did nothing. Someone's pulling his strings. He has a covert agenda."

"Holy shit," I muttered. "This just got dialled up a few more notches. The memo Mulgrave sent to this civil servant is a thinly veiled threat. Do you recognise the name?"

He leaned closer. "Christopher Craig. Yes, I do. I interviewed him a couple of times when he worked at the Home Office. He transferred to the Commonwealth and Foreign Office a few months ago."

"Makes sense. He was obviously Peter's source at the CFO. There's a printout of an email from him here – dated yesterday."

"I've never seen it."

"It must be more of the material Peter dropped in here today," I said. "It says things are worse than he thinks and he has even more damning information about Mulgrave."

"Even more damning than him deliberately letting terror attacks go ahead on British soil?" Osborne looked aghast. "What the hell is he talking about?"

"I don't know, Miles, but it can't be good."

"So, what now?"

What now, indeed. If the machinery of the state was being abused as much as this information was implying, we did not want to get caught up in its gears.

"The plan just changed," I said. "You're going to speak with Max Hargreaves at The Guardian and persuade him to run the story. I'm going to track down this Christopher Craig. He might not know it, but he's in dire need of some serious protection, plus I want to talk to him about what else he knows about Mulgrave."

"You think it's safe to split up?"

"Safer than sticking together. I'll take the dossier."

He looked anxious and started fiddling with his fingers. "But..."

"Believe me, you don't want to get caught with it. At least this way you can deny knowing the stuff that's going to earn you a bullet."

"What? You can't be serious. They wouldn't kill me over this."

"Don't be naïve, Miles. How far away is your editor?"

"Not far, he lives in Shepherd's Bush."

"And what about this Craig guy? You said you interviewed him a couple of times."

"Yes, and once was at his home in Islington. I'll write the address down."

"Just tell me, Miles. I'm not a goldfish."

THIRTY

Christopher Craig's Islington apartment was neat and modern and clean. Unlike its owner. When he opened the door at just after three in the morning he looked like an unmade bed. Messy hair, dressing gown sloppily tied and glasses balanced on the bridge of his nose at an angle. Understandable.

"You'd better come in."

"I'm not staying long, Chris."

"You said you know Miles Osborne at The Guardian."

"Depends on what you mean by *know*," I said, clicking the front door shut behind me. "We just met tonight. Judging by how easily you let me into this apartment I'd say I got here just in time."

He was suddenly ashen and reached out for the comfort of a small table in his hall. "Wildhorse."

I nodded. "I'm here to help, Chris. Not harm."

"You could be anyone."

"And I could be no one."

"What's your name?"

"My name is Bill Blake. Peter Brookline was an old friend of mine. We joined the army together."

"You know Peter at D19? Wait, you said Peter *was* an old friend."

"That's right. He was shot and killed a few hours ago by a sniper. Someone behind Wildhorse is working very hard tonight to stop things from getting out. I think we both know who that might be."

He slumped down against the radiator and cradled his head in trembling hands. "Peter is dead. I can't believe any of this is really happening. I knew I should have stayed out of it. This is a nightmare. I don't know what to do."

"Stand up, Chris. Get in your sitting room and sit on a chair. I'll make tea. We haven't got long."

*

The tea was the expensive kind rarely found in the officers' mess. In the army, the intrinsic quality of tea is measured by two metrics. If it's hot and wet, it's good tea. I took another sip and looked around his room in silence. I could see from the pictures on his walls, along with his choice of tea, that Christopher Craig was no stranger to silver spoons. Now, as we sipped our drinks in his well-appointed front room, I heard a police siren wailing in the night.

"So it's all true then," I said.

He gave a glum nod. "All true. I was Peter's source in the CFO, and he was taking information out to Miles Osborne at The Guardian. Miles was my idea. He'd interviewed me a while ago when I worked at the Home Office, but we thought I was just too close to Mulgrave to be passing material direct to journalists. Peter Brookline and I got to know each other socially some years back. I knew about

D19, although I wasn't supposed to. An elite SAS division similar to the Increment working on mostly intel jobs. I thought he was a solid middleman. It went from Mulgrave's office to me, from me to Peter and from Peter to Miles Osborne."

"And now that ratline has been busted wide open."

He looked like he was going to be sick. "So it seems."

I finished my tea and set the dainty bone china cup down on the table. I was acutely aware of time running out and the net closing in on me. "I told Osborne to talk to Max Hargreaves tonight and push him to print the story as fast as we can. Later today, if possible."

"Is this the only way?"

"It's the only way we stay alive."

"This is some sort of nightmare."

"No, it's real life. Stay focussed."

"I am focussed, damn it! I just had an operative from the SAS march into my flat in the middle of the night in a tattered, torn old trench coat with blood all over the sleeve and tell me one of my friends was shot dead."

"Take it easy, Chris. And it's a barn coat."

He finally managed the hint of a smile. "Fine, a barn coat. What the hell are we going to do?"

"You've done your bit," I said. "You've confirmed to me in person that this is really happening. That Michael Mulgrave has been turning a blind eye to intel warning us of terror attacks as part of some agenda running under the name Operation Wildhorse, right?"

Another nod. "All true. Mulgrave allowed the terror attack to happen as part of Wildhorse and as the leader of D19, Peter Brookline wanted to shut it down. For that, Mulgrave decided to clean everything up and distance himself. He decided to kill two birds with one stone by having D19 kill Zakharova. She was dangerous. She was on the outside and had been liaising with Peter about Wildhorse. The intel warning Mulgrave had come through her. If Mulgrave could frame Peter for her murder he could discredit D19, destroy Peter's credibility and bring the whole thing crashing down."

"Thanks, Chris,"

"One more thing," he said. "I never got the chance to tell Peter, but yesterday I got hold of some information from inside Mulgrave's office. My contact, whom I will not name under any circumstances, told me that there's more to come out about Mulgrave. Something seriously nasty."

"Osborne and I read something along those lines in the dossier. Any idea what it might be?"

He shrugged. He had started to turn green with panic. "Worse stuff. Much worse than turning a blind eye to the terror attack at Docklands."

I blew out a deep breath. "It's hard to imagine what that might be."

"I agree. I don't think I want to know."

"Where does Mulgrave live?"

His mouth started to work up and down but no words came out. Eventually he said, "You can be thinking of going there?"

"Is he at Carlton Gardens?"

"That's his official residence here in London," Chris said. "And no, he isn't. He's gone back to his constituency for a few days to prepare for the upcoming election."

"That's in Norfolk, right?"

He nodded. "Just outside of Horning."

"Broads country. Nice and flat."

"You can't do this, Blake. He has bodyguards wherever he goes. They're former Special Ops guys."

"Is that a fact?"

"You're playing with fire. Just let Osborne talk Hargreaves into getting it into the paper."

"I like options, Chris."

I got up. Made sure the Saiga was still nice and comfy inside the barn coat.

"When I leave here, lock your doors, stay away from your windows and keep your phone by your side. When you read about this in the papers, you're safe."

"And if it doesn't get into the papers?"

I knew what he wanted to hear. He wanted me to throw him a lifeline and tell him there was a way out. But there wasn't. We had to make it impossible for them to kill us and there was only one way to do that so I told him the truth. "Then we're all in a lot of trouble."

I stepped outside his apartment and made my way back through the rain to the BMW. I had no plan. I was winging it. I knew I had to see Mulgrave, that part was clear enough, but then things got murky. My phone rang and when I checked the screen I saw a picture of Laura and her father.

They were tied up with gags in their mouths in some sort of industrial space. They looked terrified. Beneath the image were some coordinates and a short message from Bogdan Zadik:

COME HERE NOW OR THEY BOTH DIE.

THIRTY-ONE

Zadik's message had thrown a spanner in the works. After what happened in The Blue Hour, I was surprised he had crawled back out from this rock and come at me again. He had spirit. Either that or he was deranged, but one way or the other I couldn't abandon Laura and her father. I had got them into this and I was the only person who could get them out of it. Mulgrave had to be pushed back. Luckily, Zadik's coordinates revealed the photo's location to be in an abandoned concrete factory just outside of Felixstowe, which was on the way up to Norfolk, where Mulgrave spent long weekends in his Georgian mansion.

I drove through the dawn and crunched some ideas. I felt guilty about what had happened to Laura and Dave but I wasn't consumed by it. I was the catalyst and my actions had only expedited an inevitable collision. Men like Zadik use people like toilet paper. Sooner or later, both Laura and her dad would have vanished without a trace. At least this way, they had the chance of a new life ahead of them. The issue was ugly but it wasn't the big problem.

That was Wildhorse.

A deep sinister undertow ran beneath this covert operation and the body count was growing. I knew one mistake from me would cost me my life, but I had no choice.

If I didn't face down Mulgrave they would turn me into the proverbial rat in a maze, and I too would disappear in the night. My mind raced with doubts and fears and suspicions. Could I trust Chris Craig? Was Miles Osborne on the level? What if they had got to Max Hargreaves at The Guardian and flipped him over like a soft egg? He could turn on Osborne and bring us all down.

A single, enormous chimney stretched up into the breaking dawn and split the cold blue in half like a knife. This was the concrete factory, abandoned years ago for cheaper labour in China's Jiangsu Province. A great, filthy sprawling mess of nineteen-sixties architecture coated in mould, slime and graffiti drifted into view as I pulled around a shallow bend on the approach road. All dark and no sign of Zadik – not even any cars.

But it was a big site.

I drove across the former staff car park. Faded white lines divided the parking spaces and weedy plants punched their way through crumbling water-damaged sections of the tarmac. Broken bottles and dented cans were strewn here and there and I saw the scorch signs of at least one fire. Looked like the local wildlife came here for a few bevvies after work, but not tonight. Not unless Zadik had already dispatched them.

I killed the engine near the support struts of a cement bin and climbed out of the car. A gust of cold wind whipped across the fields to the east and clawed over the site. I felt it scratch my face like nails and pulled up my collar against it. Then, I turned and walked into the factory. True, Zadik and his men could have been outside anywhere on the site, but with temperatures like this I made the call he'd want to get here early and that meant escape from this wind. Plus, the picture had been taken in what looked like an inside space.

But a concrete batching plant is a big, serious place. It's full of big, serious equipment like tilt drums and aggregate batchers and cement silos. Some of that stuff was here tonight. I'd already seen what I thought was the side of a collection hood in the photo Zadik kindly sent me. Mostly, the factory was empty of this stuff, probably taken away by the receivers years ago as they tried to squeeze every last drop of value out of the foundering company they had acquired to asset-strip.

I made my way through the shadows, tracking alongside the end of a conveyor. The rest of it was outside and a shaft of moonlight pitched in from the slit at the top. I crouched and dipped below some metre-wide pipes running up to some sort of radial press and that's when I heard them.

They were talking in Romanian and standing around a fire one of them had put together in an oil drum. Warming their hands by the flames with shotguns over their shoulders as calm and cool as if they were at a scout camp. A battered and bruised Luca was there, and Stoica and Sorin, too. One or two others whose names I didn't know, and Zadik. He was wearing a long black trench coat and his throat was obscured by a thick, black scarf. He tipped his head back and laughed at a joke. Confident, but furtive eyes peering into the dark corners of the plant.

I saw Laura and Dave behind them. They were still bound and gagged and by the look of a series of collection hoods above them, they were still in the same location. The hoods were part of the plant's extensive dust collection system and situated in front of a rusty blue weigh hopper under which Zadik was keeping his hostages. Or bait – because that's what they were to him. Bait to catch a bigger fish – the man who had burnt down his farmhouse and shot up his club.

The situation was not easy, but it was manageable. I still had the Glock, the Saiga and a dozen shotgun shells but they were armed with similar weapons. Plus they had two innocent civilians in the firing line so the first order of business was to split them up. I knew Zadik would never leave his hostages unguarded, so I picked up a chunk of concrete and hurled it off to their left. It crashed down into the top of a rotary vane feeder and cracked their night wide open.

They jumped in their skins and talked in rapid Romanian. Shotguns were whipped off shoulders like it was a competition. Zadik pulled a Makarov from an appendix holster concealed under his long cashmere coat. He walked backwards over to Laura and Dave, never once taking his eyes off where he had heard the noise. He shouted in Romanian and then Stoica gripped his Saiga and padded off towards the feeder, maybe sixty or seventy feet away. Luca limped behind him in his leg cast.

I made my way around to the feeder, Saiga still inside the barn coat. Tracking them off to my left, I moved silently over the concrete floor and then pulled a blade from the inverted sheath on my tactical vest which I was wearing under the coat. Knives are tools, not weapons. Tools do a job. SAS operators usually choose their own knives. Fairbairn-Sykes fighting knife is a good, tried and tested model. You use the right tool for the job. I've used M9 bayonets in the Iraqi desert. I like Kukris in the jungle. I have an old chute knife I sharpen on a worn-out whetstone. Tonight's job, the Connaught Square raid, required a simple commando dagger and what's good for the goose is good for the gander.

Or in this case two ganders.

Stoica and Luca were still padding about in the dark near the rotary feeder with only a pocket torch for light. Stoica wandered off. Luca shone the little torch down on the floor and found the concrete chunk I had hurled and then craned his neck up to look at the roof. A big mistake. As he angled the beam up to see where the chunk had fallen from, I made my move.

Which was too bad for him.

THIRTY-TWO

Taking a man's life is no simple thing. When I darted out from the shadows of the concrete mixer and wrapped my hand over Luca's mouth, I had no doubts about what must happen. The hand over the mouth silenced his screams, and the dagger cut the artery in his neck. The blood pressure drop was instant and he was gone. I let him slump to the floor, kicked his weapon away, relieved him of some shotgun ammo and then moved around behind the other end of the mixer. When Stoica came back from his investigation, he saw the disarmed corpse of his brother on the floor and hesitated. He didn't know what to do for a full ten seconds.

That was also too bad for him. I came out from behind the twin-shaft mixer and killed Stoica Antonescu in the same way. I didn't want his Saiga, either. A man can't use two shotguns, but I took all of his ammo as well, including a brand new alliance armament thirty round drum and tossed the weapon inside the vane feeder to stop anyone else using it. Then I moved back around to the main section where Zadik was pacing around the drumfire. Another man he named as Grosu was looking unnerved. Sorin also looked unsettled and was calling out in the direction he had watched his men wander off in.

No reply and then hurried conversation in panicky Romanian.

Easy enough to take the three of them out with the Saiga, but not with Laura and Dave sitting trussed up under the hopper. A tactical retreat was in order. And elevation. I turned and went back outside, walking over to the giant gantry crane. On my way up the manhole ladder, I took out my phone and found the picture Zadik had sent me. Then I hit reply.

"Well, if it isn't the stranger in the big leather coat."

"How're things, Zadik?"

"For you, not too good."

"If you're looking for Stoica and Luca, they're both dead. You'll find their bodies south of your current position behind one of the cement mixers."

He paused. "If they are, they deserve it."

"There's no if about it. Let Laura and her father go, now, or you've seen your last sunrise."

"Big words."

"I'm outside, Zadik. Why not come out and make me eat those words?"

I was at the top of the gantry crane now just about at the limits of the Saiga's range. When the shells were gone, I still had the Glock as a backup. I wedged myself in between the main girder and the trolley and rested the phone on the side of another steel girder and put it on speaker. Then I brought the shotgun up into the aim. The main entrance was just beyond the end of the crane's cantilever, and I had it covered waiting for their appearance. Grosu came out first. Then

Sorin arrived, holding Dave Thompson in front of him as a human shield. Zadik was last out, using Laura in the same way. The Makarov was gone and he was holding a shotgun. By the looks on their faces, they had found Luca and Stoica.

"You still there, stranger?"

His voice was thin and raspy on the speaker as the wind whistled over the gantry crane.

"Let them go, Zadik. Both of them, now. Send them over to Stoica's BMW. I parked it up under one of the cement bins. When I see them leave safely, I'll let you live and be on my way."

"And if I refuse?"

"You'll die here today, and so will the other two. We've already been over this."

"No. That's not how this is going down. I have your two friends with guns at their heads. I will count to ten and you will come out with your hands in the air or I will kill the father. Then if you are still in hiding I will count to five and kill the girl. One…"

"Last chance, Zadik."

"Two…"

The problem was the Saiga's accuracy over fifty yards. The Glock was in the same ballpark. Taking a shot at either of the men holding the hostages could get ugly over a distance like this. I wasn't taking that risk, but the third wheel was a solid target. I swept the gun around to Grosu, fixed aim on him and fired. The shell blasted a smoking hole in his chest and blew him off his feet as the explosion echoed around the plant like a peel of thunder.

185

Zadik and Sorin reacted differently. Zadik tightened his grip on Laura and pulled her back inside the factory while Sorin panicked and released Dave. The haulage driver turned and threw a punch and struck the Romanian in the face. It was well-aimed but he was in the way of my getting a clean shot off. Sorin was on the ground now, down on his backside but with the gun still in his hand. He pulled it across his body and took aim at Dave.

The old man froze on the spot. Never faced with the barrel of a gun before, he tried to reason with the gunman. He extended his arms and held his arms out in supplication. I knew Sorin would have none of that. I turned the gun on him and fired off a second shell, blowing the left side of his skull off in a mist of blood and brains and bone fragments.

Dave staggered back and brought his hands to his face. Then he doubled over and threw up all over the tarmac. I was already halfway down the manhole ladder by the time he had pulled himself together again and all the way over to where he was standing a minute later.

"You did this?" he asked.

"He was going to kill you..." "But, I never saw anything like..." He covered his mouth again.

"Dave, Zadik has Laura. He took her back inside the plant when I took Grosu out."'

"I know. He's going to kill her, Blake!"

"Not while I have a heartbeat, he isn't. Go back to the car, Dave. It's parked over there behind that cement bin."

186

He looked down at what was left of Sorin. The bleeding had stopped and a pool of congealed, black blood was reflecting moonlight. "What are you going to do?"

"End this."

THIRTY-THREE

Inside the factory and I took immediate cover behind the end of the conveyor. The moon had climbed higher into the sky and was now directly above the long Perspex skylights. Shafts of silver light shone down at narrow angles and lit the plant up in black and white.

I heard Laura scream and then the sound of a slap. Then Zadik called out to me, "Drop your gun and come out into the open with your hands in the air, stranger! Do it or I kill her. You know I will."

I made it to the end of the conveyor, following the sound of his voice. I saw him walking Laura through the shadows behind what looked like an industrial jaw crusher. He was a pace behind her with the gun's muzzle pushed in between her shoulder blades. Passing beneath the crusher frame now, they slipped out of sight.

I fired the shotgun into the air. Zadik turned and aimed his weapon at me. He fired and missed.

"Get down Laura!" I called out.

She heard me and dropped to the floor, leaving Zadik exposed. I fired a second shot over thirty yards. Some of the shots made contact with his shoulder, ripped the fabric into shreds and spun him around on the spot. It wasn't enough to take him down. He fell back against the crusher's jaw plate and brought the gun up, firing in my direction from the hip like a twenties gangster. For this reason, his aim was all over the place. I moved to cover before he got lucky and saw Laura had got up and was sprinting for the safety of the rotary vane feeder where I had taken out the Antonescu brothers.

I tracked her to the cover position and then fired on Zadik again, striking the flywheel of the crusher and spraying the drug lord with a ricocheted shot. He bolted, spinning away around the side of the crusher with his coat-tails flapping out behind him.

I gave chase, gun raised into the aim and keeping myself in between him and Laura.

"Stay where you are, Laura."

No reply. She was scared.

I was still hunting Zadik, closing in on him in the darkness of the plant. He was in here somewhere and it was only a matter of time before I flushed him out.

Let the dog see the rabbit.

I saw something – a shadow – flash inside a doorway behind the powder treatment section. Gun still raised, I made my way to the door using a line of cement kilns for cover. At the last kiln, the final ten yards had no cover. I left the kiln's protection and headed to the door. A sign over the top said I was entering the hydraulic room. Then, Zadik spun around in the doorway and fired on me. I hit the deck and tucked the Saiga up against my chest and rolled away from the incoming fire.

He kept up the barrage but I exited the roll and slammed up against the hydraulic room wall and fired on him. No time to aim and the shot missed and blew a chunk of the door frame into powder and sent Zadik scuttling inside the room for cover.

Up on my feet and into the room, firing into the darkness to keep him pinned down wherever he had hidden. I fired a ton of lead shot through the air, muzzle flashing like a strobe light as I advanced into the room. He appeared from behind a large metal cylinder and fired on me again. The light flickering from his muzzle was subdued thanks to a flash hider, but in the darkness of the hydraulic room, I was still able to track him as he moved. He was making his way over to a series of large steel suction pipes and then slipped out of another door.

I followed him into a new section of the plant. Another, smaller gantry crane loomed above me, and large vertical storage silos were standing in a neat line along the far wall. Zadik was trying to reach one of the plant's fire exits. He wanted out. I took aim and advanced on him. "It's over, Zadik."

He turned and fired from the hip, missing me by a country mile. "You're a dead man, stranger!"

I fired a second sustained fusillade at him as he darted through the silos' shadows and emptied the entire mag. I tossed the detachable mag down by my boots and smacked in Luca's drum replacement. Last one. Thirty twelve gauge shells but there was Mulgrave to handle so I had to pace myself. And the drum had drawbacks in the field, mostly the way it affected the balance of the shotgun, but for tonight it would rise to the challenge.

I kicked the empty mag away and raised the gun into the aim. My breathing was too fast and heavy, so I worked on that as I tracked his position along the silos and over to the base of the internal gantry crane. In the background, I heard a *chang-chang-chang* as Zadik dumped the rest of his mag into the darkness in a vain bid to keep me away. He was desperate and confused. He was used to hunting easier game. Men who crumpled and broke and begged before the party even started.

Tonight was a different game.

He reached the fire door and hit the panic bar. Jammed. Too bad. I took another shot from thirty yards, peppering the door panel with shot and making him almost jump out of his skin and drop his weapon. I seized the advantage and loosed another shell as an incentive to leave his gun on the concrete. He took the hint and bolted again, turning to his only escape, the internal gantry crane.

There was a chance he still had the Makarov tucked away so I kept myself behind one of the silos as I raised the barrel and tracked him up the crane. At the top, he found the handgun. He was running beside one of the crane's fixed rails now, still gripping the pistol in his hand but looking lost and dazed. He hauled himself up on top of the crane's runway, at least eighty feet above the ground, and was crawling towards the hoist. He stopped and looked up, measuring the gap between the top of the hoist and one of the skylights. Maybe he could get away on the roof, he thought.

I didn't think so.

He reached up towards a piece of plastic hanging down from the skylight above his head. I was further away than when I fired the other shots but this time the target was stationary. The shot peppered his chest and throat and he tumbled backwards off the crane. He fell through the air with a blood-curdling scream and smacked into the concrete with a wet smack.

I walked over to him at the base of the crane. He was just hanging onto life, semi-conscious and mumbling. Blood everywhere and broken arms and legs akimbo. I guessed his back was wrecked beyond repair. He looked up at me, moonlight lighting the fading life in his eyes, and gave a bitter laugh.

"You're good, stranger. I'll give you that."

I aimed the shotgun at his head. "Life's not for everyone, Zadik."

The shot killed him instantly.

THIRTY-FOUR

The drive to Norfolk was quiet and tense. From the looks on their faces, I decided against a joke about Stoica not needing his car anymore, so maybe instead one of them could have it. Humour was a strong part of my life in the regiment, but Laura and her father weren't troopers on their way back to base after a covert exercise. They were normal people with normal lives who had somehow got tangled up in the web of a major league drug dealer. Seeing men die right in front of them, violently, would take a long time to process, and even longer to reconcile.

We made good time, arriving at Norwich before lunch. I found a neat, generic hotel on the outside of town, no cameras, and checked all three of us in. I took a shower and grabbed some food and then snatched forty winks on the couch in front of the TV. It was a sports show and nice and easy to sleep along to. When I woke it was dusk and Laura and her father were watching the local news. The main story was the shooting at the concrete factory, but the details were sketchy. The chosen narrative seemed to be a shootout between rival gangs. There was no mention of their nationality and no names.

Dave gave his daughter an anxious glance and then looked at me. "Will they come after us?"

"Who?"

"The police."

"Not at all. There's nothing to link you to anything that happened there. They'll write it off as gang warfare and move along. They don't like to dwell on serious crime reaching into places like this, especially if it's international cartels."

"What if you're wrong?"

"I'm not. Just relax. You can get on with your lives now. No more Zadik, no more Sorin, no more Antonescus." I'd got up from the couch and was putting on my coat. Then I checked the Glock and the Saiga over, replaced the drum mag with a regular one and told them to stay where they were until I came back.

"So where are you going?" Laura asked. "Zadik and his gang are all dead."

"Wildhorse," I said quietly. "I'll be back before midnight."

"Are we safe this time?" Dave asked.

"Yes, but I need to do something to make sure I'm safe, too."

Laura understood. "Good luck, Bill."

I gave her a quick smile, walked outside, opened the car door and slid the shotgun down on the passenger seat. Then I climbed in beside it and switched the engine on and swerved the Beamer out of the hotel car park.

*

Cruising along the back roads into the broads, I turned up the radio and listened to some music. The vast, empty flatness of this place stretched out on either side of the car all the way to the horizon. Above them, an enormous sky was filled with stars. England was a small place and driving was often a long, hard headache, but out here reminded me almost of the American west, or my time in the Australian outback. The roads were mostly quiet and easy. On some of the longer stretches, I'd had a chance to push back into my seat and relax and enjoy the drive and think.

I understood why Dave was so nervous about going back to a normal life. Sometimes life can be so bad for so long it's almost impossible to believe it's okay to be okay again. I've felt that. I've also felt the shock he and Laura got tonight when they saw those drug dealers meet their maker. I've been there, too, like the week my wife died. These things hit you out of nowhere. When that happens you have nothing to cling to in the wreckage, nothing to swim towards. Sometimes you make it home safe, sometimes you don't.

Zadik had learnt about that tonight, and so had the rest of his gang. As I pulled off the road and headed up a dark, unlit, unsealed track, I thought about how Sir Michael Mulgrave, the British Secretary of State for Foreign and Commonwealth Affairs and third most powerful man in the United Kingdom was about to learn it too.

But first I wanted answers.

Mulgrave's ancestral home was Saltmarsh House, a large, six-bedroom Georgian country property and former vicarage. It was a listed Grade II property in Norfolk red brick with sash windows and a pretentious neoclassical portico in front of the sweeping gravelled drive. Tonight, the moon was shining on its pantile roof and a sharp frost was settling on the extensive surrounding grounds.

I parked up and gained access to the property via a small piece of woodland to the west. Now, I was crouching in the dark of night and waiting for some clouds to blow across the sky and obscure the moon. I needed the open ground between the forest and the house to be much darker if I was going to get across unobserved. Mulgrave's security detail was two SAS men. I thought there was a good chance I might know both of them.

Darker now, I pulled the Glock out and fitted my suppressor to it and made my way closer to the house. I had spent some time studying the CCTV cameras and exploiting their blind spots was not difficult. Thanks to some extensive renovation work on a brick and glass orangery to the west side of the house, coverage was blocked by scaffolding and only partial. Better still, my extensive training and years of experience in the regiment, plus comprehensive involvement in the organisation of providing security for dignitaries gave me all the knowledge I needed to make a successful ingress.

It was time for the endgame.

THIRTY-FIVE

The windows were old with small lead-lined panels no bigger than six square inches. I put one in with the Glock's grip and reached in and clicked open the catch. Inside and gun raised into the aim. This place was the heart of Wildhorse and not the place to get caught with your trousers down. I made my way down a corridor and headed towards the main sitting room. Swinging around the door and sweeping the muzzle across the room, I saw no one there so moved on to the billiard room next door. Nothing there either. In the kitchen, I found my luck.

And Sergeant Rollins.

The big man who had betrayed me in Connaught Square was working on Mulgrave's protection detail. No surprises there. I guessed Gilmore would be around here someplace too. Probably not grazing in the refrigerator for snacks, like Rollins. From my position in the door, all I could see was the back of his head as he leaned into the icebox and rummaged around for something to pass a long, boring night in the sticks.

"No ice for me, thanks."

He jumped, cracking the back of his head on the top of the fridge, cursed and spun around. As he rotated his upper

197

body he tried to bring the submachine gun hanging around his neck up into the aim but I was already on it.

"Gun on the floor and kick it over to me."

He obeyed.

"Good. Hands nice and high, please. Put the milk bottle down on the floor and step away."

"You stupid bastard."

I glanced over my shoulder and made sure the corridor was clear then turned back to Rollins. "Do it now."

He made a quick assessment and saw my finger was on the trigger. He knew I'd have a bullet in the air before he could get his backup weapon out of its holster and up into a firing position. He lowered the milk as ordered and stepped away.

"Who killed Peter Brookline?" I asked.

He was silent.

I said, "Gilmore then."

"I thought you were supposed to be clever," he said. "Coming here tonight was a big mistake, Bill."

"I know we like to keep things informal in the regiment, Rollins, but in your case, I'll make an exception. I'm a half-colonel and your CO. You call me sir."

"I'll call you dead."

"I don't think so, Rollins. Where is Mulgrave?"

"You've got to be kidding."

"Tell me or I shoot you now. And not dead. I'll start from the bottom and work my way up."

"Colonel Blake would never shoot an unarmed man."

"Too bad you've got a P226 in your shoulder holster."

The suppressor kept the noise of the shots to three muffled thuds. A double-tap to the chest and one in the forehead. Classic Mozambique drill and goodnight Rollins. He crashed back into the open fridge and knocked a jug of milk over onto his head. He was already dead by the time the milk poured down over his face and shoulders.

I knew Rollins well enough to know he would never tell me the location of the foreign secretary. Letting info like that out wasn't in the regiment's DNA. He chose his side when he signed up to Wildhorse and betrayed everyone and everything dear to him. His country, his regiment, his CO.

Across the kitchen and I took his radio and moved up a narrow flight of wooden servants' stairs. I followed it to the top where it opened out on a corridor running around the upper part of the house. Unlit, dark and cold, it gave access to a number of small box rooms once used as servants' bedrooms and was now filled mostly with junk and old papers. At the end of the corridor, I expected to find another staircase. When I found it, I checked it was clear and descended. This time the journey was shorter. The first staircase had taken me up to the top of the house, now this one was leading me down to the second floor.

I tipped my head past the doorframe and saw Gilmore. He was standing guard outside a room halfway along the corridor. Submachine gun in his grip and steady and solid on his feet. I pulled back into the stairwell, keyed Rollins's radio and thumbed SOS into it. I heard the message instantly repeated on Gilmore's radio. He spoke into the mic and asked Rollins to resend the signal.

I didn't.

Gilmore pulled his weapon up and turned and walked towards the stairs. He hesitated and glanced back at the door. He didn't want to leave his post. He spoke into the radio again. "What's up, Rollins?"

I stepped back into the stairwell and put my gun into the barn coat's big square pocket. When he turned into the stairwell, his face registered my presence with a look of shock and he pushed his finger through the trigger guard. It was too late. I smacked the gun's muzzle out of the way, drew my arm back and drove my clenched fist into his face, aiming a good twelve inches behind it. Powering the hard bone of my knuckles through his nose as if it was made of warm butter, I heard a wet smacking sound as the cartilage exploded in a cloud of mucus and blood vapour. His head cracked back against a wooden panel and nearly knocked him out.

Dazed with the speed of the attack, he toppled over and collapsed to the floor. He was down and out for the count, but still the faintest glimmer of consciousness glowed behind his eyes as they rolled up into his skull. D19 don't recruit men who stop halfway through the job, and now I propelled my boot into his head, kicking it back with such venom and power I almost snapped his neck. Then I reached for my suppressed Glock and fired three shots into the T-Box zone in the middle of his face.

"That's for Peter," I muttered as I lifted the Glock once more into the aim and made my way along the corridor to the room he had been guarding. Nice and slow, easy soft tread. Big riot boots crushing the Persian runner. I listened at the old oak door. Nothing. I had to go in quick. Gilmore would not have been posted here to guard nothing. Mulgrave was in this room, maybe sleeping. I crooked my elbow and brought the gun up level with my head and prepared to kick the door in.

"Drop the weapon, Bill."

I felt the cold steel of a handgun's muzzle push into the base of my skull. Worse, I recognised the sound of the voice.

"Good evening, Mark. I thought you were in Wiltshire tonight."

Major Mark Shepherd reached around and took the Glock from my hands, patted me down and removed the Saiga from my coat pocket. Then he pushed me closer to the door with the gun stull pushed into my skull. He moved with the cautious, safe actions of a man handling a wild animal, and he was wise to do so. We both knew what happened to traitors.

"Nice and easy does it, old man," he said.

I said nothing. It was hard to find the words. I'd known Mark since selection.

"We're going in to see Sir Michael now, and you're going to play nice or I'll kill you where you stand."

THIRTY-SIX

"Ah, it's none other than Lieutenant Colonel William J. Blake, VC, SAS."

"I prefer Blake. Friends can say Bill."

"Let's go down the middle then, Blake. I was expecting you."

Shepherd pushed me into the room. Sir Michael Mulgrave was sitting in a leather studded armchair beside a roaring fire in the corner. More dark hardwood panels. Civil War-era paintings of the cavaliers and roundheads in battle. Neatly trimmed houseplants. Vaulted ceiling. I had only ever seen Mulgrave on TV, usually at the dispatch box in the Commons. He looked smaller and older in the flesh.

"You seem to have crashed my party," he said coolly and turned his phone over in his hands.

Shepherd moved the gun from my skull and stepped gingerly away from me, taking himself to the other corner of the room but keeping the weapon trained on me at all times. When he got there, he set the Saiga down on a side table and pulled my Glock from his pocket and put that beside it. Then he took a seat. "And we have so much work to do, too. It's all very tiresome."

"And what work might that be?" I asked.

Mulgrave looked at Shepherd. "Tell him, Mark. There's no need to worry."

"Sir Michael is a patriot, Bill. Like me. Like you. He believes this country is going to the dogs and he wants to do something about it."

Mulgrave said, "When Mark says it's going to the dogs, he speaks with the typical understatement of the well-bred British Army officer. It's a toilet bowl, and it's time someone acted to change things."

"And that someone is you," I said.

"Cometh the hour, cometh the man."

"And what exactly are you doing about it, besides turning a blind eye to foreign terrorists butchering our citizens on British soil?"

"Wildhorse is an extensive programme, Bill," said Shepherd. "Its remit ranges far beyond merely turning blind eyes to foreign terrorists."

"I don't understand."

"The people are asleep, Blake," Mulgrave said. "They're sleepwalking into oblivion. Aggressive foreign powers are building blue water navies while our people play computer games. Foreign spies operate with impunity in our towns while our people get drunk and watch asinine television programmes. Fundamentalist terror organisations kill our people on their holidays, or worse, they come right here into the homeland and do it right under our noses."

"And how is you turning a blind eye to the Docklands bombing helping any of this?" I asked.

"It's waking them up!" he snapped. "The more devastation and butchery they see, the faster they will wake up. Don't you understand?"

And then I got it. "You can't be serious. You're personally behind some of the recent terror attacks."

"Yes."

"You're not just ignoring allies' intel when they give you a heads up about a terror attack, you're actually committing some of these acts yourself."

"Yes."

"Good God."

"If we don't wake the people up soon it will be too late!" he said. "They see their own children blown apart and do nothing. It's time all that changed. It's time they woke up and got angry, and I'm going to make sure it happens. With enough terror, not only will they start to understand the problem but they'll demand a strong leader to bring them out of the night and into the day. The PM is weak and has no stomach for a fight. He's terrified of polls and statistics. He hides behind his spin doctors. This is my time, now."

"Was the Luton bombing yours?"

"Yes," Shepherd said. "And the Liverpool one before it. When the Russians tipped us off about the Docklands, it was a great opportunity to get a result without any organisation or effort."

"You're insane. Both of you."

"Come off it," Shepherd said. "And you can climb down off that high horse of yours, too. We both know you've done some terrible things in the name of Queen and Country."

"Always following military orders and always legitimate military targets."

"The line blurs sometimes."

"No, it does not," I said. "And this is why I never joined the intelligence services. I'm a soldier, and I fight only other soldiers. I thought you were the same."

"Can't you see Sir Michael is right?" he said. "This country is finished if someone doesn't take the initiative and do something."

"What I can't see, is how a man I thought had integrity and honour could breathe the same oxygen as this creature right here."

"It's irrelevant what you think, Blake," Mulgrave said coolly. "You're not with the programme and you're supposed to be dead anyway. Grant and Brookline are both dead, as are Bentinck and Wainwright and we have teams scouting for Osborne and Hargreaves at The Guardian as we speak. Good teams. They've already taken Christopher Craig out of the equation."

"You've had Craig killed, too?"

"Of course not, he killed himself in a tragic suicide about an hour ago."

"You bastards."

"And Osborne and Hargreaves will both be dead before dawn. Why not join us?" Shepherd said, earning a sharp scowl from Mulgrave. I guessed this development had never been discussed. "We could do with a man like you."

"You know me, Mark. You knew the answer to your question before it left your lips."

"That's too bad," he said. "Because there's nothing else for you. You can't go back to the regiment. Brookline is dead and D19 is over – shut down in disgrace. You're a rogue. You're an outlaw. There is no way out of this mess for you."

"No, there is not," Contempt ran through Mulgrave's voice like hardened steel. "He's not coming over to us, Mark. Kill him. Kill him, now."

THIRTY-SEVEN

Shepherd hesitated. It was a mistake, but faced with a direct order from such a high-ranking government minister and killing his old friend in cold blood, he had understandably frozen. Only for a second but it was enough. I dived to the floor and rolled behind Mulgrave. Shepherd cursed himself and fired at me. The gun exploded in the peaceful study and buried a nine-mil round in a portrait of Oliver Cromwell. I pulled on the back of Mulgrave's chair and tipped it over, crashing him onto the rug by the fire. Shepherd was up out of his chair and aiming at me again.

I picked up the leather armchair. Heavy, solid and old and hurled it into Shepherd. He fired and the chair caught the round then it smashed into him and knocked him to the ground. Mulgrave was behind me, terrified and unsure what to do. I lunged towards Shepherd, pulled the chair away from him and kicked the gun out of his hands and punched him in the face. His head bashed against the rug hard. He grunted in pain and pulled his arm back and curled his hand into a fist ready to take a swipe at me.

Movement behind me. Mulgrave was on his feet.

I reached out for the side table and snatched the Saiga, turning on Shepherd and aiming. He raised his hands, palms out. "Please, no."

"Time to return to unit, Shepherd."

One shot to the head and he was gone. Mulgrave went white and staggered backwards. Then he saw the gun I had kicked out of Shepherd's hand and went for it. He snatched it up greedily and held it at arms' length. It wobbled around in his clean, pale hands like it was made of jelly.

"You get back."

"Be honest," I said coolly. "You didn't think it was going to go this way tonight. Am I right?"

He was inching away from me, eyes occasionally settling on the mutilated corpse of Mark Shepherd. His last line of defence against the sharpest operator in D19. He moved slowly until his back brushed up against a large bookshelf.

"Stay away from me."

And then he was gone. The bookcase was a panel leading to a secret passage. Not at all uncommon in English country houses of this era. I was unfazed. Lifted the Saiga up and went into the passageway. Dark, narrow, lit with naked light bulbs. I just caught sight of Mulgrave's back as he scuttled around a corner and I gave chase.

I followed the passage to a set of wooden steps leading up to a trapdoor in the roof. Again, not uncommon in old houses. They have large roofs and require lots of maintenance. Many have family flags that need raising and lowering for various reasons. Saltmarsh House was no exception. A large, glorious flag flapped in the moonlight, emblazoned with the Mulgrave coat of arms. Just beyond the flagpole, the family's scion was stumbling across the galvanized steel flashing, Shepherd's service pistol waving absurdly in the air.

I followed him across the roof to the west wing where a stone balustrade ended his journey. Beyond it, a fall of over one hundred feet to the gravelled drive. Now, the gun came back around into my face.

"I will kill you, Blake."

"Put the gun down, Foreign Secretary."

"You can't win, you know. Back when you came into the study, I sent a message to someone. I did it the instant I saw your face. I know who you are and what you're capable of. I'm no fool. That's why I sent the message to Quartermain. You know Quartermain, don't you, Blake?"

Jack Quartermain was an old Royal Marines commando I had worked with in the distant past. Another old bootneck like Gilmore. Up from the ranks to sergeant, he was easily the hardest man I had ever known and the only man who had ever bettered me.

"Yes, I know of him."

"I'm sure you do. Mark Shepherd introduced me to him. He left the service a few years back due to PTSD and alcohol issues. All patched up now. Mostly. He came to work for me and Wildhorse."

"That's nice. Does he do your ironing, too?"

Mulgrave said, "No, he kills people. I sent him an emergency code and I know he has received that code. Just one single word. The word is *Taipan*, the most venomous land snake on earth. It's found in central Australia but for our purposes, it's a codeword that tells Quartermain you have escaped from custody and are on the loose."

"I'm flattered by the analogy."

"He *will* kill you," he said, his voice almost a whisper. "The only way you can hope to have any kind of normal life free of the constant threat of death is if I call him off. I can do that now. Just throw the gun down and join us. Join Wildhorse. Everything you have done tonight can be forgotten."

"I don't think so, Mike."

He bristled at my use of his first name. "Last chance, Colonel Blake. Lower the gun or Quartermain will retain his orders to kill you. No matter where you go, what you do, you can never sleep again."

"It's no deal, sorry."

"You can't expect me to roll over, Blake. I'll go to prison for the rest of my life for treason."

"You're not going to prison, Mulgrave."

We looked at each other for a second. A sharp wind blew in from the North Sea and whipped over the broads and cut across us like razor blades. Our faces were lit by the cold moon, and we both knew what I had meant.

He moved first, lifting the heavy gun. He was trying to raise it so he could see through the sights and make sure his aim was good. Before the gun was halfway to his line of sight, I fired the Saiga repeatedly, unloading the rest of the magazine into him and blasting him over the balustrade and off the roof. I just stood there and waited for his body to hit the gravel. Smoke twirled up from the Saiga's muzzle brake before being caught by the wind which now lifted a lock of my hair and the front panel of the old leather barn coat.

When I heard the smack and crunch of Mulgrave's shot-ridden body impacting on the gravel, I slung the shotgun over my shoulder and headed back to the roof hatch.

THIRTY-EIGHT

Driving east to the coast, a big fat red sun was climbing right over the road. I pulled down the visor and blocked the light out, then tuned the radio until I got a news station. There was lots of talk about a fire somewhere in Manchester, and then an item about rising knife crime in London. The woman reading the news had a smooth, calm voice. She was about to hand over to the weather report when she paused and then announced some breaking news.

She was saddened to tell listeners about the sudden, shocking death of Sir Michael Mulgrave, whose body was found in his Norfolk home earlier today. Police were not treating it as suspicious, which was polite society's way of saying he killed himself. A statement from his distraught family implored people to stay away and respect their privacy at this difficult time.

"I'm not going to ask what you did when you left the hotel last night," Laura said.

"You already know." I pulled the car up and turned off the engine.

"Yes."

"I knew two of them," I said. "Two of the security detail."

She frowned. "You knew them, and yet you killed them?"

Her voice trailed away. It's a little known fact that the Norfolk Broads are manmade. Way back in the twelfth century, the people from around here used to come and dig the peat out for fires. They'd burned through most of the local wood and turned to the peat. Two centuries later the sea levels rose and filled in the pits they had dug. It was still early and the sun was low. I watched a pink-footed goose wheel in the sky and drop down below the rushes of Salthouse Marsh. I'm a details man. I like detail. I pay attention to detail – detail like the goose calling out from the reeds. But Laura was still there, sitting beside me and quietly waiting for an answer. She had come out with me to the coast to say goodbye. Now, I didn't know what to tell her.

"They were the men who betrayed me in London at the start of this nightmare," I said. "Gilmore and Rollins. They were in Mulgrave's pocket from the very beginning. They got what was coming to them. I took no pleasure in it."

"I couldn't live your life," she said at last, glancing at the time on her phone. "Dad should be here soon."

"Tell him to stay in the car when he gets here. I don't want to talk to him. No more thanks."

She typed out the message and sent it. Her father had been back at the hotel, packing their meagre belongings into a bag and preparing to start a new life without Zadik. Now, we climbed out of the car and watched the sunrise over the North Sea, a cold disc of grey steel that daubed the muted mustards and olives of the local saltmarshes with watery light. Clouds heavy with water scudded above a bitter easterly wind which whipped over the crashing tides and

213

dunes and scratched at my face. I winced and pulled up my collar. Exhaustion clawed at me like a wild animal. I was bruised and cut and wounded, and I wanted a bed and twelve hours sleep.

Instead, I knew I had nothing but an endless road ahead of me.

"You'll be all right now," I said.

"I hope so. What about you?" she asked, reaching out for my hand. "Will you be okay?"

I smiled at her. "Don't worry about me, Laura."

"It's been a wild ride, Blake," she said, her face breaking into a grin. "You sure you won't stick around? I think Dad could do with a new driver."

Now I grinned too. "I don't think that's for me."

A taxi pulled up behind us and the driver sounded the horn. Dave was sitting in the front seat beside the driver. He gave me a simple wave and I nodded once in response. Laura was already putting her phone in her bag while I was climbing into the driver's seat and turning the ignition. She picked up her bag by the straps and slung it over her shoulder. Swept some hair away from her face as she leaned down into the open window. The sun lit up her hair, yellow as April hay in the early dawn light.

"So, this is it," she said.

I nodded.

"Where are you going?"

"I have no idea."

"You don't even know where you're going?"

"They can sometimes be the best journeys. What about you?"

"When I've helped Dad get his business back up and running again and I've got my head straight, I think I'm going to go back to college. They run night classes for adults. Start my life again."

"Don't go too fast," I said. "Chasing your dreams is usually better than catching them."

She thought about that for a while. Then, she leaned over and kissed me on the cheek. Before I could speak, she walked away. Turning halfway to the waiting cab, she looked me in the eye with half a smile on her lips. "Goodbye, Bill Blake."

Then she was gone and so was I.

AUTHOR'S NOTE

This is an old idea of mine, going back originally to 2004. I put it aside to work on other projects and not being one to rush ideas, I didn't pick it up again until 2017, mentioning it on my blog in January 2018 as the story about 'a man named Blake'. I worked on it again for a few weeks, and then put it down to focus on the Jacob crime thrillers and another series of adventure thriller books, The Hunter Files. If you enjoyed this novel, please consider leaving a short Amazon review. Thank you.

Website: www.robjonesnovels.com

Facebook: www.facebook.com/RobJonesNovels/

Email: robjonesnovels@gmail.com

Twitter: @AuthorRobJones

Printed in Great Britain
by Amazon